"Funnier than *Il Trovatore.*"

—B.N. Hare
Editor-in-Chief

P.G. WODEHOUSE

If I Were You

INTERNATIONAL POLYGONICS, LTD.
NEW YORK CITY

IF I WERE YOU

PREFACE

The Wodehousian sagas of Jeeves and Bertie (and the Drones who bumble about them), of the Blandings Castle crowd (democratically bridging the gulf between earl and pig, with intellectual honors about even at opposite ends of the span), of Mr. Mulliner's friends-and-relations (as varied in personality if not in genera as Rabbit's), of the Oldest Member's gallery of duffers and scratch men ("scratch women" is too coarse a term to be employed in that gentlemanly world), stretch on for book after book, for decade after decade; and for many readers, the sagas *are* Wodehouse. If they encounter someone they like in one book, they expect to find him or her in another and another and another, and usually they are not disappointed.

The sagas indeed have such vitality that they sometimes cross-pollinate. Bertie Wooster's unsettling but (or hence) short-tenured girlfriend Bobbie Wickham is a connection of Mr. Mulliner's; Bertie's weedy newt-fancying friend Gussie Fink-Nottle drifts into the roiled waters of Blandings, recalling the narrator of Poe's "Descent into the Maelstrom" unwittingly courting his fate; and others have walk-ons in series not their own.

But there are a great many Wodehouse one-shots, universes (or anyhow serviceable stage sets) created for one story only, then struck; actors engaged for one spirited performance then melted into air, into thin air. This would seem to arise from Wodehouse's insistence on happy endings: once the boy has got the girl, all's well, but nothing as interesting is going to happen to them afterwards. In the sagas that doesn't matter very much, as the star- (and often aunt-) crossed lovers are secondary to the series heavyweights: Jeeves and Bertie, Emsworth and Galahad, Ukridge and Corky. Once they get to the conclusive clinch, they are conclusively escorted from the stage. A few brace of them may encounter obstacles and be allowed a reappearance in a subsequent installment, but this is usually indulgence on the author's part, or perhaps the exercise of economy—Wodehouse may have been reluctant to let even secondary characters depart entirely while there was still some comic value left to them, much as thrifty gum-chewers used to retrieve a *bonne-bouche* from the bedpost in the morning to extract the last of its flavor.

In the Wodehouse romantic novels, though, the ones in which the lovers are the leads, not juvenile and soubrette, the final curtain really is final. You can badly want to know how Packy Franklyn and Jane Opal prospered when *Hot Water* had cooled or whether that Small Bachelor George Finch ever learned to address his mother-in-law as anything chummier than Mrs. Sigsbee H. Waddington; but if so, want, as any of a number of Wodehouse nannies might have said, must be your master.

Thus in the present book we have some of Wodehouse's most pungent creations — it is a tossup between Ma Price and Syd on the one hand and Sir Herbert and Lady Bassinger on the other for placement in the Top Ten Deplorable Duos in the canon — who bloom but once and are remorselessly discarded. They exist to complicate the lives and love of Tony and Polly, so that once those twain become one, the others' occupation's gone, and there's nothing to write about them, any more than about the happy and therefore uninteresting pair. (In *Their Mutual Child* [*The Coming of Bill* in England], Wodehouse did deal with a marriage, and a distinctly troubled one at that. Reading it suggests that his instinct to drop the curtain on the clinch was a sound one.) We also have a distinctly piquant ending situation, the destiny of the Price tonic being in itself enough to claim the attention of those who respond to the romance of commerce; and how Tony and the Bassingers sort out their convictions concerning the roles of nature vs. nurture in determining character presents unending possibilities — possibilities which, though not beyond all conjecture, can be conjectural only.

Some readers have perceived *If I Were You* as dismayingly snobbish, with its depiction of Syd as the Cockney outsider impinging on the well-bred world of the Bassingers. In fact, any kind of close look reveals the book as completely subversive of respect for the class system, particularly the hereditary aristocracy. (This is not surprising, as the only people Wodehouse seems to have admired as classes are writers, composers and cricketers.)

The literary economy touched upon earlier extended to Wodehouse's reading as well as to the characters of his invention. Like Shakespeare, he felt that if So-and-so hadn't gotten the most out of a plot, well, P. Grenville Wodehouse would supply the lack. And, also like Shakespeare, there was no pretense to the audience that the plot was all his own work. *If I Were You* will remind extremely wide-reaching readers of W. S. Gilbert's "The Baby's Revenge" in *The Bab Ballads.* If it does not, the lawyer, Weatherby, points it out for them, as indeed does Tony. The ballad's lines

> Give me the pounds you've saved, and I'll resign
> My noble name, my rank, and my condition

are at least approximately, if not precisely, applicable to the story. Readers who know "The Baby's Revenge" should be assured here that *If I Were You* ends far more happily, with nobody *in extremis* or even Madeira.

Gilbert was in no position in 1931, when the book appeared, to express any opinion on Wodehouse's use of his dramatic contrivance (which was anyhow not really his, as the poem is a burlesque of a common melodramatic situation), having died some decades earlier. However, he did survive long enough to entertain (not quite the *mot juste,* as it turned out) a very young PGW at a dinner at his house. The experience would not have disposed him to oblige Wodehouse in any way whatever.

Gilbert, a domineering raconteur, launched into quite a long story, apparently meant to be funny. When he stopped speaking, Wodehouse, who knew his duty as a guest, burst into hearty, whinnying laughter, though he didn't quite see the point. The other guests followed his lead, but Gilbert—who had paused for enhanced effect just *before* the punch line, which could now never be delivered—turned his basilisk glare upon Wodehouse alone.

At that moment, Wodehouse might well have wished to resign his name, his rank and his condition, or at least his place at table, in favor of almost any other situation. Who can say that this experience may not in the fullness of time have resulted in the Gilbertian-flavored *If I Were You?* Only those with no penchant for the preposterous, among whom surely are to be numbered very few readers of this book or others by its author.

D. R. Bensen

D. R. Bensen, a noted Wodehousian scholar, has edited several volumes of the Master's works.

TO
GUY BOLTON

Chapter One

THROUGH the wide French windows of the
drawing room of Langley End, the country seat
of Anthony, fifth Earl of Droitwich, in the
county of Worcestershire, there was much to be
seen that was calculated to arrest and please
the eye. Beyond the smooth gravel drive which
swept out of sight round a hedge of rhododen-
drons lay a velvet lawn, rolled and tended
through the centuries by generations of assidu-
ous gardeners. This ran down to the tree-fringed
lake, and where the water ended woods began,
climbing in an unbroken mass up the hillside.
Most people who came into the drawing room
stood at one of the windows and stared devoutly,
silently drinking in the lovely scene.

Not so Charles, Lord Droitwich's footman.
All this was old stuff to Charles. Besides, he was

answering the telephone. Its ringing had interrupted him as he set out the tea things.

"Hullo?" said Charles. "Yes, this is Langley 330. Who are you? . . . Who?"

Slingsby, the butler, entering behind him, eyed him disapprovingly. Like all butlers, he considered that answering the telephone was a task that called for a skill and address beyond the scope of mere footmen. You wanted a butler for it, and a good butler, at that.

"*Hul*-lo . . . *Hul*-lo . . . *Hul*-lo . . ."

The disapproving look deepened on Slingsby's moonlike face.

"What do you think you're doing, young man?" he inquired. "Singing a hunting chorus?"

"It's a trunk call from London, Mr. Slingsby. Someone to speak to his lordship."

"Who?"

"I couldn't hear, Mr. Slingsby. The line's buzzing."

"Give *me* the instrument."

The butler placed a large ear to the receiver with the air of a man who intended to stand no nonsense.

"What is it, please? . . . Speak up, can't

you? Place the lips close to the . . . Oh, the *Daily Express?*"

"*Daily Express?* What do you suppose *they* want?"

Slingsby was not a man who invited chat from underlings. He jerked his thumb authoritatively; and Charles, rebuked, withdrew.

"No," said Slingsby, addressing his distant interlocutor, "I am not Lord Droitwich. I am his lordship's butler. . . . His lordship is in the garage and cannot be disturbed. . . . Nor can I answer questions regarding his lordship's private affairs. If it is true, I have no doubt his lordship will notify *all* the papers in due course. . . ."

Up to this point, the butler's manner had been a model of all that was stately and official. He now suddenly unbent and became startlingly human.

"Hey!" he cried. "Don't ring off. What won the two-thirty?"

A sound behind him caused him to look apprehensively over his shoulder. A woman of early middle-age had come through the French window. He recognized, without pleasure, his employer's aunt, Lady Lydia Bassinger. Lady

Lydia was smartly dressed, as for a feast or festival. She had, as a matter of fact, just returned from the local flower show.

"What is it, Slingsby?"

"The *Daily Express,* m'lady. A London periodical. Ringing up to ascertain if there is any truth in the rumour, current in the metropolis, that his lordship is engaged to be married."

"What!"

"Yes, m'lady."

"I'll talk to them," said Lady Lydia.

She took the receiver from the butler's reluctant grasp.

"Hullo, Freddie," she said, as she did so.

"Hullo," said the exquisitely turned-out young man who had just entered. He wandered to a table and picked up an evening paper. "Somebody phoning?"

"Yes. The *Daily* . . . Hullo? Are you there? . . . What?" An expression of mingled surprise and indignation came into Lady Lydia's face. She turned for sympathy to her nephew. "There's a lunatic at the other end of the wire who keeps calling me Little Bright Eyes."

"I fancy the wires must have become crossed, m'lady." It was Slingsby who spoke, and he spoke like one in mental agony. "If your lady-ship will permit me . . ."

Lady Lydia resisted his attempt to recover the telephone. She was listening. And, as she listened, a grim look appeared in the eye which she turned on the shrinking butler.

"Oh? . . . I see . . ." She covered the receiver with her hand. "Does it mean anything to you, Slingsby, that Little Bright Eyes won the two-thirty race at Gatwick? Tomato, second. Bashful Yankee, third. What were *you* on?"

The butler gulped disconsolately.

"Fruit Salad, m'lady."

"Ass! Finished nowhere."

"Yes, m'lady."

"What half-wit gave you that?"

"Master Frederick, m'lady."

The Hon. Freddie Chalk-Marshall looked up from his paper.

"Sorry, Slingsby. These things will happen."

"Serves you right," said Lady Lydia severely, "for believing what Master Frederick tells you. I hope you lost a packet."

"Yes, m'lady," said Slingsby, and left the room, to be alone with his grief.

Lady Lydia turned to the telephone again.

"Hullo . . . Are you there? . . . Forgive my brief inattention. I was talking horse to my butler. Now that we have concluded the stable chat, I may tell you that you are speaking to Lady Lydia Bassinger, Lord Droitwich's aunt. My husband was Lord Droitwich's guardian during his minority. Eh? What? No, I don't think so. I feel sure that, if he had taken so serious a step, he would have mentioned it to me. I have lived with Lord Droitwich for ten years, ever since the death of his parents, and . . . Hullo . . . Oh, have you gone? . . . Well, good-bye."

She hung up the receiver and sank into a chair.

"Heavens!" she said. "I'm melting."

Freddie looked out at the gardens, glowing in the midsummer sun.

"I thought you would find it a bit warm," he said. "How was the show?"

"Much the same as usual. We got an Honourable Mention for calceolarias."

"Three cheers," said Freddie. "And rousing ones, to boot. What *is* a calceolaria?"

"Oh, just one of those calceolaria-looking flowers. I never know one from the other."

"I see. You're back a bit early, aren't you?"

"We are," said Lady Lydia. "Your uncle said he felt faint and thought he had sunstroke. Here he comes now—the fraud."

A red-faced, horsey-looking man, about ten years older than Lady Lydia, had tottered into the room. His gorgeous costume and glistening top-hat drew a striking tribute from Freddie.

"My God!" said Freddie. "Great Lovers Through the Ages!"

Lady Lydia surveyed her moist husband witheringly.

"Come in—skrimshanker!" she said.

Sir Herbert Bassinger mopped his forehead.

"I'm not a skrimshanker! I tell you I did feel faint. Who wouldn't—at a beastly flower show in morning clothes and a blasted top-hat? I'm nearly dead. It was over a hundred in the shade."

"You shouldn't have stayed in the shade," said Freddie.

"What I want to know," proceeded Sir Herbert, shrill with self-pity, "is why *I* get dragged into these affairs every year."

"The family must be represented, ducky," said Lady Lydia.

"Well, why doesn't Tony represent it? He's the head of it. Am I Lord Droitwich or is he? Where *is* Tony? Loafing in a hammock somewhere, I suppose."

"On the contrary," said Freddie. "In the garage, wrestling in prayer with his two-seater."

Lady Lydia nodded thoughtfully.

"That settles it. He *can't* be engaged to Violet Waddington. If he were, he would be wherever she is."

"She's having a bath," said Freddie.

Sir Herbert stared.

"Engaged? What's all this about being engaged? Who says he's engaged?"

"The *Daily Express* seems to think so. They were on the telephone about it just now."

"Eh? What? Why?"

"My fault, I fancy, Uncle Herbert," said Freddie.

"Yours?"

"Yes. You see, young Tubby Bridgnorth has just had his annual row with his guv'nor—this time because he very tactlessly kidded the old man about the way he was going bald. Unpleasantness ensued, and Tubby is now in the metrop., trying to earn an honest penny as a gossip writer.

I thought it only matey to tip him off about Tony's engagement, so I sent him a wire just after lunch."

"But, you poor nincompoop," said Lady Lydia, "Tony *isn't* engaged."

"Oh, yes, he is."

"Did he tell you?"

"No. But I saw him kissing Violet in the rose garden."

Lady Lydia uttered a feverish exclamation.

"In the rose garden? Ye gods! And you call that evidence! Didn't your mother teach you *anything* about the facts of life? Don't you know that everybody kisses everybody in rose gardens?"

"How do *you* know?" asked Sir Herbert jealously.

"Never mind!"

Freddie raised a soothing hand.

"Don't worry," he said. "This was one of those special kisses . . . *lingering* . . ."

"Ah?" said Lady Lydia dreamily. "One of those?"

"Besides, I could tell from the look on Tony's face."

"Rapturous?"

"Half rapturous and half apprehensive. Like you see on a feller's face when he's signing a long lease for premises that he knows he hasn't inspected very carefully."

Sir Herbert puffed meditatively.

"Well, I hope you're right, by Jove! Think of Tony married to the heiress of Waddington's Ninety-Seven Soups! Whew! It's like striking an oil gusher!"

Lady Lydia was still doubtful.

"I don't want to damp your pretty enthusiasm, Herbert," she said, "but I confess I should feel easier in my mind if he had kissed her somewhere else except the rose garden. I know those rose gardens."

"Oh?" Sir Herbert was moist, but not too moist to bridle at this remark. "Well, let me tell you that, when I was in my prime, I knew just as much about rose gardens as you do. Let me tell you . . ."

"Later," advised Freddie. "Later, I would suggest . . . unless you want to include old Wad in the audience."

Sir Herbert followed his nephew's glance.

"Oh, ah," he said, and fell to polishing his top-hat. The door had opened, and a short, burly man was coming in. A man who looked as if Nature had intended him to wear mutton-chop whiskers and who seemed to be refraining from that outrage on the public weal only with an effort.

G. G. Waddington, of the Ninety-Seven Soups, was beaming.

"I say, everybody!" he said. "Heard the news?"

Lady Lydia started.

"You don't mean . . . ?"

"Yes, I do. Droitwich and my little Violet."

"Now, perhaps," said Freddie, "you'll believe a feller."

"They're really engaged?"

"Had it from Violet's own lips. Met her on the stairs just now."

"Capital!" said Sir Herbert.

"A most delightful surprise," said Lady Lydia.

"Surprise?" Mr. Waddington's manner was waggish. "Oh, come, Lady L.! Who was it who suggested . . ."

"Yes, yes, Mr. Waddington," said Lady Lydia hurriedly. "We won't go into that now. Here is Violet."

Violet Waddington was tall and slender and as hard-boiled as a fashion plate. She seemed to have got her looks from her mother's rather than her father's side of the family, for she was as undeniably beautiful as the sponsor of the Ninety-Seven Soups was not. Her manner was languid and blasé.

"My dear!" said Lydia. "Your father has just told us the news."

"Oh, yes?" said Violet.

"I'm delighted," said Lady Lydia.

"Thank you."

"I'm delighted."

"Thank you, Sir Herbert."

"And *I'm* delighted," said Freddie.

"Thank you, Freddie. I'm glad," said Violet, with the faintest suspicion of a stifled yawn, "that you're all pleased."

"The thing being now official," said Freddie, "I suppose I'd better compose another thoughtful wire to young Tubby."

He moved to the writing desk and, taking a chair, settled down frowningly to literary composition. Lady Lydia was still fluttering round the bride-to-be, as if hoping to raise the scene to a rather more emotional and enthusiastic level than it had touched at present.

"It's what I have been hoping would happen, for ever so long. I'm sure you will be happy."

"A splendid fellow—Tony," said Mr. Waddington.

"Best fellow that ever stepped," agreed Sir Herbert.

"Oh, yes," said Violet, with that same air of being compelled to join in the discussion of a rather tedious topic. "And I will say this for him—he knows what to do in a rose garden."

Sir Herbert coughed.

"He inherits *that* from his aunt," he said, in the nastiest possible manner.

A gleam came into Lady Lydia's eye.

"What was that, Herbert?"

"You heard," said Sir Herbert with dignity. He made for the door. "I'm going upstairs to take off these infernal clothes."

"Yes," said Lady Lydia. "Get your maid to put you into something loose, and we'll discuss that last crack of yours."

Freddie had risen and was ringing the bell.

"I missed that," he said. "What crack?"

"Never mind," said Lady Lydia. "But let me tell you this. No port for your uncle Herbert to-night."

"Now, there's a thing," said Violet, "which, as an experienced married woman, you may be able to tell me. How do you keep them off the port?"

"Violet!" said Mr. Waddington.

"My dear," said Lady Lydia, "you won't have to worry about that with Tony for years. At present, he's much too concerned with keeping himself fit."

"Yes," said Violet, with another faint yawn. "He *is* a bit of a bally athlete, isn't he?"

Slingsby loomed in the doorway like a dignified cloud bank.

"You rang, m'lady?"

"*I* rang," said Freddie. "Has the car gone round to the garage yet, Slingsby?"

"Not yet, Master Frederick."

"I want Roberts to take a telegram down to the village for me. Where is he?"

"In the kitchen, Master Frederick."

"Right-ho," said Freddie, and departed, bearing the telegram which was to gladden the heart of his young friend, Tubby Bridgnorth.

Slingsby turned to Lady Lydia.

"I beg your pardon, m'lady."

"Yes, Slingsby?"

"In the matter of Price, m'lady."

"Oh, yes. She's coming here to-day, isn't she?"

"Yes, m'lady." The prospect seemed to intensify the butler's customary air of melancholy. "Accompanied by her son. Your ladyship kindly gave me permission to entertain them in my pantry this afternoon. I now understand that they will 'ave a young person with them, m'lady—she 'olds the post of manicurist in young Price's shop."

"That's all right. The more, the merrier."

"Thank you, m'lady. What I was about to inquire was whether it would be permissible to allow the young person to roam about the gardens? It would be a treat for her. I understand that she comes from America, where, as your ladyship is aware, they don't 'ave 'istoric places like this."

"That will be quite all right, Slingsby."

"Thank you, m'lady."

The butler withdrew, rather in the manner of an ambassador who has delivered a protocol— or whatever it is that ambassadors do deliver. Violet Waddington turned to Lady Lydia.

"Price? Is that Tony's old nurse that he was telling me about?"

"Yes. Slingsby's sister. She married a barber in London. And I wish to goodness," said Lady Lydia, with sudden irritation, "that she would stay in London, where she belongs."

"Don't you like her?"

"She gives me the creeps."

"Why?"

A sudden gloom seemed to have settled on Lady Lydia Bassinger.

"She's a nasty old thing," she said, "and she drinks too much. Well, I'm going to imitate Herbert and change into something human. Will you start tea?"

"All right, Lady Lydia. Tea, Father."

For some moments after the departure of their hostess, there was silence between the Waddingtons, father and daughter. Violet had busied herself at the tea table, and Mr. Waddington was standing at the window, looking out at the lawn and the lake. There was a frown on his face. And that this was not caused by anything which had displeased him in the scenic surroundings of Langley End was made plain by his words, when at length he spoke.

"I must say," he observed, turning and directing at his daughter a glance of reproof, "I don't know what girls are coming to nowadays."

"Meaning what?" asked Violet.

"I may be old-fashioned," proceeded Mr. Waddington, warming to his subject, "but *I* like to see a little enthusiasm on these occasions."

Violet sighed. She frequently found her father trying.

"Why be sentimental?" she said.

"Why *not* be sentimental?" retorted Mr. Waddington.

"I'll tell you why not," said Violet. "Because you know and I know that it's simply a business deal. I provide the money, Tony supplies the title. Do let's be honest. You brought me down here to land Tony. And I've landed him. I don't see any need to gush about it."

A spasm shook Mr. Waddington.

"Hush!" he said. "You *know* walls have ears!"

"And *you* know that you and Lady Lydia stage-managed the whole thing. Propinquity . . . Those moonlight strolls . . . Getting Bertie Smethurst down here to act as pacemaker . . ."

"Don't *talk* like that!" cried Mr. Waddington, in agony.

Violet dropped a lump of sugar in her tea and stirred it placidly.

"I tell you," she said, "when he proposed to me, I felt the whole thing was like shooting a sitting bird."

"Stop it!"

"Of course, if you really insist on enthusiasm, I'll do my best. Oh, Father dear," said Violet girlishly, "when Tony asked me to be his wife, I was so taken aback and so completely flabbergasted to think that he should feel that way about *me* that I simply gasped. He's a perfect lamb, and I'm awfully, terribly in love with him. I wouldn't mind if he hadn't a title or anything. All that annoys me," she added, resuming her normal manner, "is that it was so darned *easy*."

Mr. Waddington choked down his indignation. Experience had taught him that in verbal argument his child was scratch and he a mere twenty-four-handicap man.

"Well, easy or not," he said, "you've done it. And now I'll phone the papers."

"Not here, if you don't mind."

Mr. Waddington paused en route for the telephone.

"Eh?"

"I don't want to sit listening while you boom out the glad tidings. Do it from the pub in the village."

"Oh, all right," said Mr. Waddington. "All right, all right, all right. Your ladyship is dashed particular, I must say. Just one thing," he continued, pausing impressively at the door. "You aren't the Countess of Droitwich yet. If you want to be, I'd recommend you to be careful how you talk when you're with Tony."

"Why, Father!" cried Violet. "You don't suppose that, when I'm with Tony, I *talk?* I just simper shyly."

"Bah!" said Mr. Waddington.

It was not much of a last word, but, such as it was, he had it.

Chapter Two

FOR some minutes after the speaking of this last word, Violet Waddington had the drawing room to herself. She ate cucumber sandwiches placidly and was engaged upon her third when the Hon. Freddie Chalk-Marshall, having delivered his telegram to the chauffeur, returned in search of sustenance. Freddie liked his drop of tea of an afternoon.

"Hullo," he said. "All alone?"

"Yes," said Violet. "Lady Lydia has gone up to change her dress, and Father's on his way down to the Droitwich Arms."

"To have a spot?"

"No. Just to telephone the papers about the latest fashionable engagement."

Freddie frowned.

"Oh?" he said. "Bit tough on young Tubby.

I'm afraid he'll miss his scoop. You haven't met young Tubby, have you?"

"No."

"A good chap, but too prone to kid his old guv'nor. Talking of the old boy, I'm trying to sell him a new hair lotion."

"I didn't know you were in the profession, Freddie."

"Just trying to make a bit of the filthy. This was some stuff that Tony brought home from London a month or two ago, and it struck me as pretty good. He got it at young Price's barbershop. It's made up from an old recipe of Price's grandfather's. It seemed to me that, if I could interest capital, I might be in a position to touch Price for a stiffish agent's fee. You never know."

"The Prices are coming down here this afternoon."

"Oh, dash it!" said Freddie. "Are they? She used to be Tony's nurse."

"I know."

"A ghastly female. And the son's worse. A highly septic little bounder."

"Well, I don't suppose you'll meet them."

"Not if I see them first," agreed Freddie. There was a pause.

"I say," said Freddie.

"What?"

"When I was outside, I spotted old Tony on the horizon. Heading this way. Due any moment, I imagine. Do you want me to clear out or anything?"

"Of course not."

"Well, I know what you young couples are. Still, if you say so . . ."

The sound of footsteps on the gravel drive caused him to break off. A large body appeared in the middle of the three French windows. Anthony, Lord Droitwich, in person.

"Tea!" he cried. "In the name of the Prophet, tea!"

"Hullo, Tony," said Violet. "You seem warm."

"I *am* warm. I was an ass ever to have started fixing that bally tin kettle on a day like this. I've got to drive down to the village in a minute to get a battery."

The fifth Earl of Droitwich was a massive young man on the borderland of thirty. A portrait of him over the mantelpiece showed that he could look, if not handsome, at least clean and attractive; but at the moment he did not appear at his best. He was in his shirt-sleeves, and was both dishevelled and hot. A wisp of fair hair hung over a forehead that was marred by more than one spot of motor grease, and there was dirt on his forearms.

His appearance drew censorious comment from his younger brother.

"Tony," said the Hon. Freddie, more in sorrow than in anger, "you look foul."

Lord Droitwich had paused in front of a mirror, and he seemed to consider that the verdict, though harsh, was just.

"Pour me out a brimming cup, dear, will you?" he said. "I'll be back in a second."

He disappeared, to return in a few moments clean and tidy as to the hair. He was still in his shirt-sleeves, for he had left his coat in the garage. But then he had never been the fastidious dresser his brother was. Indeed, the Hon. Freddie had long since given him up with a sigh as a bad job, considered from a sartorial point of view.

He took the cup which Violet handed him and drained it at a gulp.

"More," he said.

Violet refilled the cup. Tony drained it again and seemed to feel better. He lit a cigarette.

"Has Freddie heard the news?" he asked.

Violet nodded.

"How did he take it?"

"You could have knocked him down with a feather."

Freddie intervened solemnly.

"I say, Tony."

"Hullo?"

"If you want to kiss her," said Freddie, "smack into it. I don't mind."

It was a generous invitation, but before either of the interested parties could avail themselves of it their attention was diverted by an unpleasant noise on the drive outside. A vehicle of some kind was approaching. Freddie, who was nearest the window, looked out. Tony, peering over his shoulder, uttered an exclamation and drew back.

"Oh, dammit!" said Tony.

"Don't say it's callers," said Violet.

"Not for you. It's Ma Price."

"Don't *you* like her, either?"

"She gives me the heeby-jeebies," said Tony. "She will insist on bursting into tears and kissing me. A dashed, damp, disturbing process, believe me. I can understand anyone crying at the sight of me. I can just understand some eccentric person wanting to kiss me. But the two at the same time—no. It's contradictory."

He drank more tea to fortify himself for the ordeal. These periodical visits of his old nurse were a trial to Lord Droitwich. If he had ever really enjoyed the society of Ma Price, he must, he felt, have been easily pleased as a baby.

"She's brought her son with her, I hear."

Freddie moaned softly.

"Will *he* kiss you?" asked Violet.

"Certainly not," said Tony. "To kiss a member of the peerage would be foreign to Syd Price's principles. He's a Socialist."

"The consignment, I noticed," said Freddie, "also included a dashed pretty girl. Who would she be?"

"She's the manicurist."

"How do you know that?"

"Slingsby was talking about her." Violet got up. "Well, I'm going to stroll casually past the back premises and have a look at them," she said. "A woman who survived kissing Tony as a baby is worth inspection."

"I understand I was a singularly handsome and lovable child," said Tony.

"Coming with me?"

"I've got to get my battery."

"Well, if I meet Mrs. Price, I'll tell her you're waiting eagerly for that kiss."

"But would prefer it dry this time."

"*Sec,*" said Violet. "All right. I'll try to arrange it."

The door, closing behind her, swung open again, and Tony rose and shut it. He came back to the table, to find his brother staring before him in a curiously fishlike manner that somehow made him feel ill at ease. He took a slice of cake, a little embarrassed. There was something rather portentous about Freddie Chalk-Marshall at this moment, and Tony did not like it. Freddie frequently gave his elder brother the sensation of being a mere babe in the presence of a veteran man-of-the-world.

He broke the silence.

"Well, Worm?"

"What ho, Reptile?" said Freddie.

There was another pause. Tony felt that he must know the worst at once. If his brother disapproved of his engagement, let him say so and put him out of his suspense.

"What do you think of the situation?" he asked. "Violet and me. All right?"

Freddie weighed the question with the solemnity of a high priest consulted by an acolyte.

"Well . . . yes . . . and no," he said.

"That's lucid. What do you mean?"

Freddie flicked a speck off his coat-sleeve. The gravity of his manner increased.

"Well, I suppose you know," he said, "that, as your future father-in-law, old Wad will now become entitled to slap you on the back in all places?"

"That's true."

"I'll tell you one thing," said Freddie, not unkindly but firmly, "if he thinks I'm going to take him round and introduce him at Buck's, he's vastly mistaken."

Tony looked thoughtful.

"Yes," he said, "I admit old Waddington is a shade over the odds. But, putting that on one side, you think I'm a lucky man, don't you?"

Freddie regarded him with kindly pity.

"Do you want me to speak frankly?"

"I do."

"From the bonded storehouse of my knowledge?"

"I do."

"Well, then, I suppose you know," said Freddie, "that you've been had?"

Tony·digested the unpleasant word in silence. "Had?" he said.

"The whole thing's been a put-up game."

"Don't talk rot."

"Not rot, old boy."

"Are you trying to make me believe that a girl like Violet would run after a chap like me?"

"Dear old bloke," said Freddie, "does a mouse trap run after a mouse?"

"Until this afternoon I didn't dream the thing would happen."

"She did."

Tony was losing the repose that stamps the caste of Vere de Vere.

"You know all about it, don't you?" he said rudely.

"Anthony Claude Wilbraham Bryce," replied his brother, "I know all about everything.

They call me Frederick the Infallible, because
I am never wrong."

"You make me sick."

"Oh, I wouldn't take it too hard, old boy,"
said Freddie equably. "Rather a compliment,
really. Shows you have a market value."

"Bah!"

"Anyway, it's done now. By the way, hearty
congratulations! I think you will be very, very
happy—perhaps."

"What do you mean—perhaps?"

"Nothing, old boy, nothing. Just 'perhaps.'"

The heated reply that trembled on Tony's
lips remained unspoken. Looking past his
oracular brother, he was aware of a new arrival.

Standing in the French window was a young
man of his own age. He wore knickerbockers,
and a small and rather horrible moustache dis-
figured his upper lip. In his demeanour were
blended the impudence and sheepishness char-
acteristic of the Cockney who has strayed from
his own familiar ground and is in surroundings
foreign to him.

" 'Ullo!" said this young man. He smiled a
furtive smile. "Sorry. Didn't know there was
anyone 'ere. Good-afternoon, m'lord."

Chapter Three

Tony was taken aback, and he found it difficult for a moment to divert his mind from the
interrupted conversation. But, like the good fellow he was, he succeeded in putting aside his
uneasy thoughts regarding Violet and addressed
himself to the task of making the intruder feel
at home.

"Why, Syd," he said, "I didn't recognize you
for the moment. Come on in. You know Syd
Price, Freddie."

"'Ow do, Mr. Frederick?"

"Pip-pip," said Freddie austerely.

"We saw you pass the window," said Tony.
"How's your mother?"

"Not so good, m'lord. 'Ad one of her spells
on the way down. It's 'er 'eart."

"That's bad. Has she taken something for it?"

"Yes, m'lord. About a flask-full."

Tony turned to Freddie, whose manner, he considered, was too plainly that of one who desired it clearly to be understood that he was no party to this degrading scene.

"Ma Price's heart is not strong, Freddie."

"Really?" said his brother coldly.

"Never has been, has it?" said Tony perseveringly, to Syd.

"No, m'lord. I remember when Pa'd take us on a holiday—to Margate or wherever it might be—he'd never risk buying Ma a return ticket. Careful man, Pa was."

He laughed heartily. Then he caught Freddie's eye, and the laughter died away.

"I must welcome her to the old homestead," said Tony. "Is she in the pantry?"

"Yes, m'lord. You'll find her a bit tiddley."

Freddie winced. He seemed to be feeling that no good man should be subjected to this sort of thing.

"That's a pity," said Tony. "Still, she'll want to see me."

"I'm only 'opin' she won't see two of you."

"Great Scott! Is she as bad as that?"

"She's a bit tuppence, m'lord, and I won't deceive you. When Ma 'as her spells, you 'ave to shoot the brandy into 'er, regardless." He eyed Tony fixedly. "Will you pardon a remark, m'lord?"

"Go ahead, Syd."

"It's about your 'air."

Freddie raised an eyebrow.

"His what?"

"His 'air."

"He hasn't got one yet. You're peeping into Volume Two."

"I was alluding," said Syd Price stiffly, "to the 'air of 'is lordship's 'ead. I don't like the look of that 'air, m'lord. You've bin 'aving it cut by some local chap. Ah, and a rare mess 'e's made of it. Barbarians, we call these country fellows."

"Syd's prejudiced, Freddie. These London men!"

"R!" said Syd. "You may well say 'London men.' My father 'ad the shop before me." A lilt of pride came into his voice. "R! and 'is father 'ad it before 'im. And *'is* father before *'im*. I got a set of me great-granddad's razors. Wonderful-lookin' things with blades as big as bread-knives."

He addressed this tribal chant to Freddie, fixing him with a compelling eye.

"Really?" said Freddie.

"Oh, it's true enough. I can show 'em to you."

"I'll look forward to it," said Freddie frigidly.

He rose and started for the door.

"Going, Freddie?" asked Tony.

"Yes," said Freddie, with decision. "I feel a little faint. For some reason or other, I've got one of my spells."

Syd Price eyed the door darkly as it closed. He made a bitter gesture.

"It's fellers like 'im," he said, "that's 'astenin' the Social Revolution."

Tony, kind-hearted as ever, endeavoured to heal the wound.

"Oh, you mustn't mind Freddie. It's just his way."

"A way," said Syd ominously, "that'll lead ere long to tumbrils in Piccadilly and blood running in rivers down Park Lane."

Tony shuddered.

"What a beastly idea!" he said. "So slippery. But don't be too hard on Freddie, Syd. He may be a bit Eton and Oxford, but he's working in

your best interests. You remember that hair
lotion you stuck me with, last time I was at your
place? The one your grandfather invented. He's
trying to interest capital in it. He thinks it's
good."

"It *is* good."

"So at any moment you may clean up big. Remember that in Freddie's favour when you're
helping to put the Aristocracy to the sword. By
the way, when do you expect this Social Revolution to start?"

Syd smiled darkly.

"It may be to-morrow!"

"Ah!" said Tony. "Then there's just time for
me to go down to the village and get that battery. You won't mind my leaving you?"

"Go ahead, m'lord. Any objec. to me mooch-
ing around in 'ere while you're away?"

"Of course not. Fond of pictures?"

"I like these," said Syd.

He had been wandering round the room as he
spoke, and now he came to a halt beneath a portrait which hung in state on the far wall. It
represented a militant-looking gentleman clad
in armour, whose chin tilted defiance at some
unseen foe, and whose right hand, the better to

deal with that foe in the event of his starting what Syd would have described as "any funny business," gripped the hilt of a very long and presumably sharp sword. Syd gazed up at him with grudging respect.

"Who's he?" he asked.

"That's an ancestor of mine," said Tony. "Richard Long-Sword, they called him. He pulled the nose of the King of Scotland for calling him a liar and was sentenced to be drawn and quartered."

"Coo! Did he, though?"

"But his daughter smuggled a sword into his prison—the very sword he's holding there—and he cut his way out and escaped."

"They certainly went it in those days."

"Hullo!" said Tony.

"Yes, m'lord?"

Tony was staring at his visitor. Syd moved uneasily. He was sensitive about his appearance and was wondering if he had got a smut on his nose.

"That's funny," said Tony. "Do you know there's a likeness between you?"

"Me an' him?"

"Yes. A most striking resemblance."

Syd chuckled amusedly.

"Not guilty, m'lord. None of my ancestors ever knew any of your ancestors, except Ma, an' I'll take my oath *she's* respectable."

Tony laughed.

"Oh, I'm not casting any aspersions, Syd. Well, I'll leave you. If you want a cigarette, you'll find them over there."

"Thanks, m'lord."

Tony disappeared through the French window, but Syd Price, though feeling that he could do with a smoke, did not go immediately to the table where the cigarette box stood. He remained beneath the portrait, looking up at it. He assumed the pose of the portrait, his chin up and his right hand clutching an invisible sword hilt.

"Rum!" said Syd.

As he spoke, the door opened. It was Slingsby who entered. The butler's impressive features wore a worried look.

" 'Ere!" he said.

Syd came out of his reverie.

" 'Ullo, Uncle Ted."

"Where's your mother?" asked the butler.

" 'Ow should I know? Isn't she in the pantry?"

"No, she's not. She's wandering round the house, and she's got no business to."

"She won't do any 'arm. She likes to look the old place over. Didn't she live 'ere for two years when his lordship was a baby?"

"That's neither 'ere nor there. Her place is in the servants' quarters, and she's no more business roamin' the 'ouse than you 'ave in this room."

Syd Price was not fond of his uncle, and it seemed to him that the time had come to put him in his place.

"Is that so?" he said. "Let me tell you I 'ave his lordship's express permish to be in this room. And, what's more, now I'm here, I'll 'ave a cigaroot."

"You dare!"

"Specially invited to by 'is lordship," said Syd triumphantly. "Try *that* on your pianola."

The butler stood baffled.

"Impudent young 'ound!" he said.

Syd reached for his invisible sword hilt.

"Less of it, varlet, or I'll cleave thee to the chine! Yes, by my halidom!"

"Have you gone mad?"

"Only a little 'armless fun, Uncle Ted. 'Is

lordship's bin telling me I look like that josser up there."

"Oh, he has, has he?"

"Yes, he has, has he! And so I do. There's a most striking resemblance."

He eyed the portrait wistfully.

"Coo!" he said. "I wish I *'ad* bin sprung from a warrior stryne like that. I'd have made a better earl than some of them, I can tell you."

"What's that, young Syd?" said Slingsby sharply. It was impossible for a man of his ample build actually to give a start, but a sort of ripple of indignation had passed through his body. "Don't you come your Socialist airs in *my* 'ouse!"

"Your 'ouse?" Syd guffawed rudely. " 'Ats off to 'Is Grace Lord Ted of Slingsby. Meet the Duke!"

The butler regarded his nephew belligerently. He wished, for the hundredth time, that he had had the bringing up of him. The problem of what boys were coming to nowadays had often agitated Slingsby, and in Sydney Lancelot Price it seemed to him that all the unpleasing qualities of modern youth were assembled in a mass. He breathed heavily through his nose.

"I've half a mind to put you over my knee and spank you."

Syd was not a member of the Fulham Debating Society for nothing.

"That's what's been the trouble with you all along," he retorted easily, "only 'aving 'alf a mind."

In the painful family wrangle which ensued, the butler did his best. But he was up against a nimbler dialectician and was having the worse of the exchanges when he was saved from total demolition by the arrival of a newcomer.

This was a woman of mature years and a rather dishevelled aspect. Mrs. Price was wearing her best Sunday black satin and had applied to her hair some roguish unguent borrowed from Syd's stock, but she still looked subtly disreputable. Her face was red, and her eyes, which had a glazed appearance, seemed to find difficulty in focussing their objective.

However, after blinking once or twice, she contrived to sort out the contending parties: and, having done so, addressed them with severity.

"Nah then, nah then, nah then!" she said. "What's all the row about?"

Slingsby turned, not sorry to find a new antagonist. A butler of spirit does not like to be worsted in argument by a snip of a boy, and there was not much change, he realized sadly, to be got out of young Syd. Young Syd had a way of twisting your remarks and making them recoil on you like boomerangs. The result, the butler presumed, of spending half his time arguing with his Bolshie friends. He regarded his sister with an accusing eye.

"Ho!" he said. "So there you are, you aggravating old woman!"

Ma Price supported herself against a handy chair and went into the fray with the readiness of a veteran.

"Who are you calling a wo—hic!"

" 'Ullo, Ma!" said Syd. "Still a bit tiddley, aren't you?"

Ma Price bridled.

"Nothink of the kind," she said with dignity. "If I 'ad to 'ave a drop or two on the way down, whose fault was that? More to be pitied than censured, I am—with this 'eart of mine."

"Your 'eart's in the right place."

"I know it is, but it goes all jumpy. What were you two chewing the rag about?"

"Uncle Ted didn't like me sayin' I'd make a good earl."

"R! 'E little knows!"

"And I didn't like him lounging about in this room," said Slingsby warmly. "And I won't 'ave it, neither."

Ma Price eyed him owlishly.

"Maybe Syd 'as got more right in this room than what a lot of other people 'as."

"What do you mean by *that?*"

"Never mind," said Ma Price darkly. "I know what I know."

"And I know what *I* know—and that is that you've no business in 'ere. Get back to the pantry."

Ma Price released her hold on the chair in order to fold her arms haughtily. This so nearly led to disaster that she hastily resumed her grip. There was, however, a distinct implication of haughtily folded arms in her voice.

"Don't you talk 'igh and mighty to *me,* Theodore Slingsby," she said, "because I won't 'ave it. If I wanted to say a thing or two—well, I *could* say a thing or two."

"Then say it in my pantry. What do you think

this room is—a waiting room at Clapham Junction?"

Syd's manner was that of an enthusiast who has secured a ringside seat for the battle of the century.

"Come on, Ma!" he urged encouragingly. "It's your turn. Say something about his face."

But a swift change had come over Mrs. Price's mood. Tears were trickling down her face.

"I wouldn't demean myself. Nobody loves me. That's what's brykin' my 'eart."

"Cheer up, Ma."

"Me brother insults me. Me own son won't even look at me."

"I'll look at you all right, Ma, and won't charge you a penny, what's more."

"Oh dear! Oh dear! Oh dear!"

"Stow it, Ma."

Slingsby glowered.

"It's your fault," he said sombrely to his nephew, "lettin' her get into this state."

" 'Ad to give her something. She 'ad one of her spells."

"What'll his lordship think, if he sees her like this?"

The word appeared to start a train of thought in Ma Price's mind.

"I want to drink 'is lordship's 'ealth in a drop of port."

"You'll get *tea*," said the butler bitterly. "And you'll get it in my pantry, you misguided old josser. Come on, both of you."

"Where's Polly?" asked Mrs. Price tearfully.

"She went out in the Park to look at rabbits," said Syd. "Never seen one before. Not running about, that is, with all its insides in it. She'll come back at tea-time. It's what's known as the 'omin' instinct."

"She's a nice girl, Polly. American—yes," said Ma Price, as one who is not afraid to look on the dark as well as the bright side. "But I always say," she went on, "that it takes all sorts to make a world, and I will say for Polly that *I've* never found her shooting and murdering like these Americans do all the time. A most quiet, nice, respectable girl I've always found her, and never shot anyone, as far as I know."

"You can't keep Ma away from the movies," explained Syd. "She thinks everybody in America is a Chicago gorilla."

"Pulling pistols out of their 'ip pockets and

shooting at people," said Mrs. Price querulously. "I don't *'old* with it, and, if I 'ad my way, it'd be put down by law. But nobody listens to me. Not that Polly's like that, American though she frankly admits herself to be. A quiet, nice, respectable girl she is, and clever at 'air and manicurin', too. You might do worse than marry Polly, Syd. She'd make you a good wife. No nonsense about Polly. Never shot anyone."

"Not a marryin' man, Ma," said Syd austerely. "Too wrapped up in the business. No time for girls. Me scissors is me sweetheart."

"All I want," said Mrs. Price, abandoning the theme, "is a little love."

"Me, too. And buttered toast. 'Op it, Ma. You'll feel a different woman after a cup of tea."

"Where's 'is lordship? I want to fold him in me arms."

"You shall fold him in your arms all right, later on," said Slingsby, overwrought. "Come *on!* Of all the annoying, aggravating relatives a butler was ever afflicted with. . . ."

The door closed. Peace descended on the drawing room.

Chapter Four

Nor was it only over the drawing room that Peace spread her gentle wings. The afternoon had now reached that point at which, when by some accident the weather does happen to be fine in England, a sort of magic spell appears to fall upon all created things. The world seemed asleep. Shadows lay along the lawn. Birds twittered drowsily in the shrubberies. A dewy coolness was in the air, promising twilight and rest.

Into this mellow quiet the sudden uproar outside cut like something apocalyptic. In itself, it was a noise ordinary enough in these days of high-powered cars, being composed of the tooting of a motor horn, the squealing of brakes, and a startled cry: but, coming now, its effect was shattering. It sounded like front-page stuff.

Silence followed it. An ominous silence. Then

on the gravel drive there was the sound of scraping feet, and through the French window, still in his shirt-sleeves, shuffled Lord Droitwich, walking delicately, for he was bearing a girl in his arms. He looked about him, saw the sofa, and, carrying her to it, placed her against the cushions. This done, he stepped back and, mopping his forehead, eyed her apprehensively.

"Oh, my stars!" said Lord Droitwich.

She was lying back with her eyes closed. She reminded him of a wounded bird. She was a small, fragile girl with piquant features and a mouth which looked to his lordship the sort of mouth which, if it ever opened again in this world, would smile readily.

"Oh, my Lord!" said Lord Droitwich. "Oh, my aunt!"

In desperation he took up one of the limp hands and patted it vigorously. It was like beating a butterfly, but he stuck to it. And presently her eyes opened.

They were singularly attractive eyes—large and soft and the colour of very old sherry, but Tony was in no frame of mind to be a connoisseur of eyes. If they had resembled those of a codfish, he would have been just as pleased.

The only thing that mattered to him was that she had opened them.

"Hello!" she said.

Her voice was pleasant, too—low and musical and with just a suspicion of a strange inflection to make it more agreeable. But Tony, blind to eyes, was deaf to voices. He continued to mop his forehead in silence.

The girl looked about her.

"Oh!" she said, as if remembering.

Tony was regarding her with relief and reverence.

"Do you know," he said, "you're the most wonderful girl I ever met."

She smiled. He had been right about her mouth. It did fall, on the slightest provocation, into a most delightful smile.

"*I* am? Why?"

"In the first place," said Tony, "because you come up smiling after having a whacking great car run into you. And, secondly, because you didn't say, 'Where am I?'"

"But I know where I am."

Tony drew a deep breath.

"I know where I thought I *would* be," he said. "In the dock, with the Judge putting on

the black cap and saying 'Prisoner at the Bar,'
stop me if you've heard this before . . ."

"It wasn't your fault. I popped out of the
bushes right under your wheels."

"You did pop, didn't you?"

"I ought to have been more careful."

"So ought I. Tell me, do you spend much of
the summer in bushes?"

"There was a squirrel in there. I wanted to
take a peek at him. Don't you love squirrels?"

"I don't think I've met many socially."

"I've seen them often enough in Central Park,
but never really close to."

"Central Park? Oh, you mean in New York?"

"Yes."

"Do you come from New York?"

"I lived there all my life till I came over
here!"

"What brought you over here?"

"I've always been crazy to see other countries,
and I thought England would be simplest as a
start, because of the language."

"I see."

"So, when I'd saved enough for the fare, I
came over."

"Awfully sporting."

"Well, it panned out all right. I've got a good job at Mr. Price's."

Enlightenment came to Tony.

"Oh, you work at Syd's shop?"

"Yes. I'm a manicure. Do you know Mr. Price?"

"Known him for years."

"Of course. You would, wouldn't you, working here. I suppose he comes here a lot."

"Pretty often. His mother was Lord Droitwich's nurse."

"I know. It's funny to think that he and Lord Droitwich were babies together. There must have been a time when you couldn't tell them apart. And now, there's Mr. Price in a barbershop, and Lord Droitwich in this wonderful house. . . ." She broke off. "Say, listen! Won't you get into trouble, bringing me in here?"

"Of course not."

"Well, you know, I suppose. I should have thought . . ."

"That reminds me," said Tony. "I ought to have mentioned it earlier. Are you hurt?"

The girl pondered the question.

"I do feel kind of funny."

Tony moved her arm up and down.

"Does that hurt?"

"No-o-o," she said doubtfully. "But my knee does."

"May I look? I mean, knees are no secret nowadays."

"I suppose not. But be careful."

She pulled down her stocking. He inspected it gravely.

"Bit scraped. I'll get some warm water."

He went to the tea table and came back with a dripping handkerchief. He applied it gently.

"Yell if there's any agony," he said.

"It's all right." She looked about her. "What a peach of a place this is," she said. "It must be swell, working for Lord Droitwich. I hear he's an ace."

"Who says that?"

"Mrs. Price. She raves about him. She says he was the prettiest baby she ever saw. She has a picture of him lying in a sea shell with nothing on."

"Disgusting!"

"It isn't at all," she said warmly. "He was a sweet baby. Such a kind face. He isn't married, is he?'

"Going to be, I understand."

"Ah! I thought some girl would hook him sooner or later."

Tony started uncomfortably.

"What's the matter?" asked the girl.

"Oh, nothing." Tony put the damp handkerchief in his pocket and rose. The girl pulled up her stocking. She wiggled her knee gently.

"It's much better," she announced.

Tony was standing with a slight wrinkle in his forehead. He felt that a newly engaged man ought to be receiving more encouragement than was being vouchsafed to him to-day. First Freddie with his infernal "Yes . . . and no," and now this girl with her sinister verbs.

"*Hook* him, did you say?" he observed after a pause.

"For his title."

Tony achieved a wry smile. Yes, undeniably, things were being made a little difficult for him.

"You don't think it within the bounds of possibility," he asked, "that a girl might love Lord Droitwich for himself alone, as it were?"

She shook her head decidedly, and the brown hair danced about her eyes.

"Not a Society girl. I've seen too much of them. Doing their hands, you know. Of course, that was back in New York, but I don't suppose Society girls are any different over here."

"Did they confide in you, these Society girls?"

"Not what you'd call confide. But they used to talk like I wasn't there. Hard? Ask me! Grabbers, I call them."

Tony's discomfort increased.

"How exactly does a girl—grab a man?"

"Oh, flattering him . . . acting coy. . . . There's all sorts of lines. . . . Pretending to be sympathetic. . . . Playing off some other man against him . . ."

"Bertie Smethurst!"

"What?"

"Nothing," said Tony. "Just an exclamation. Merely a heart cry. Go on."

"I suppose in a place like this she would make him take her for walks in the moonlight. . . ."

Tony rubbed his chin.

"Freddie was right," he said ruefully.

"Freddie?"

"My brother."

"Does he work here, too?"

Tony laughed.

"Work? Freddie? You don't know the lad. He toils not, neither does he spin."

Her eyes widened.

"Listen," she said. "Who *are* you? You don't talk a bit like an ordinary chauffeur."

"Good-evening, your lordship," said the voice of Ma Price behind them. She hiccoughed decorously. "I've been looking for you everywhere."

The girl had jumped up. She was eyeing the recipient of her unguarded confidences reproachfully.

"Your lordship?" she said.

"I'm sorry," said Tony. "Hullo, Nannie."

"It wasn't fair!"

"I know. I'm sorry."

"Leading me on that way!"

Mrs. Price spoke reprovingly.

"Now, don't you go being saucy to his lordship, Polly. Leading you on, indeed!"

"Nannie," said Tony, "I blush to say that I did lead her on. You must have brought me up very badly."

"I'm sure, me lord," said Mrs. Price, bridling, "I gave you all the love and care that any baby could wish."

"But too little of the back of the hairbrush. With what result? I acted a lie to this young lady. A lie, I tell you. A lie. My God!"

He covered his face with his hands. Polly laughed. Mrs. Price became severer.

"You've bin upsetting 'is lordship."

"No," said Tony. "I upset her. That's how we met."

"Well, it all looks very queer to me," said Mrs. Price austerely, "and if you ask me if I like it I'll tell you frankly I don't."

She would have developed this theme, but at this moment the door opened, and Slingsby burst in.

"Oh! 'Ere *again!* Didn't I tell you . . ." He perceived Tony, and his manner lost its generous fire and became butlerine. "I beg your pardon, m'lord," he said. "I was not aware that your lordship was present."

"Quite all right, Slingsby."

"May I urge with the utmost emphasis, m'lord, that it's no fault of mine that this woman keeps popping in here every two minutes like a rabbit into its 'ole?"

"It's quite all right. We were just having a cosy little chat."

"Very good, your lordship."

Tony turned to Polly.

"By the way," he said, "have we met? My name is Droitwich—Lord."

Polly smiled her ready smile.

"Mine is Brown—Polly."

"How do you do, Miss Brown?"

"Pleased to meet you, Lord Droitwich."

They shook hands. And, as they did so, Lady Lydia Bassinger came in, followed by Sir Herbert.

Lady Lydia stopped in the doorway. Mrs. Price was not one of her favourites, and the drawing room at the moment seemed full of her. As a preliminary to rebuking what she considered the undue levity and familiarity of Miss Polly Brown, Ma Price had begun to swell formidably, and she appeared to Lady Lydia to be occupying far too much cubic space for one in her position.

"Ah, Price," she said stiffly. "How are you?"

Mrs. Price bobbed.

"Nicely, thank you, m'lady, if it wasn't that me 'eart is brykin'."

"Too bad," said Lady Lydia coldly. "You must do something about it."

"This is Miss Brown, Aunt Lydia," said Tony. "I just knocked her seventeen yards, two feet, and eleven inches with my car. A European record."

To the visitor from a far land Lady Lydia could be gracious.

"I hope you're not hurt, my dear," she said amiably. "My nephew, when he gets behind a steering wheel, is a public menace. You are the manicurist, aren't you, from young Price's shop? I must get you to look at my hands next time I'm in London."

"And if," resumed Mrs. Price, suddenly deciding to address her remarks to Sir Herbert and fixing him with an Ancient Mariner eye, "you ask *why* me 'eart is brykin' . . ."

"I don't, dash it," said Sir Herbert, recoiling.

Lady Lydia came to the rescue of her hard-pressed mate.

"Slingsby," she said, "take Price into the housekeeper's room and give her some port and anything else she wants."

"All I want is a little love and affection," the guest of honour pointed out, dabbing at her eyes with a soiled handkerchief. "Can't I 'ave a bit of a word with you, m'lord?"

"I'll come and see you later, Nannie," said Tony. It was plain to him that his aunt Lydia had had all of Mrs. Price's society that her system could support. "I've got to take my car back to the garage."

"*I* see," said the sufferer, descending further into the depths. "Your car means more to you than I do—me that's done so much for you."

Lady Lydia and Sir Herbert exchanged glances.

"Slingsby!" said Lady Lydia authoritatively.

The butler knew his place too well to throw a look of sympathy and understanding in her direction, but he puffed like one who saw just what she meant.

"Very good, m'lady." He turned to his sister. "Come on, if you please, and don't be silly."

Just as Lady Lydia, a moment before, had "picked up" the butler's eye like a hostess at a dinner party, so now did Slingsby pick up Polly's. He had not known Polly long, but he had seen enough of her to be sure that she was a girl to be relied on at a time like this.

Nor was his confidence misplaced. Obeying the silent call, Polly Brown went to Mrs. Price and, taking her arm, started to lead her off.

"Come along, Mrs. Price," she said cheerfully. "It'll do you a lot of good to sit down and have a rest."

Mrs. Price considered this. She seemed doubtful.

"Well, all right. But if I wanted to, I could . . ."

"Price!" cried Sir Herbert sharply.

The injured woman looked at him as if she were seeing him for the first time.

"Why, 'ow do you do, Sir Rerbert. I was just saying . . ."

"Never mind what you were just saying," interrupted Lady Lydia. "Lord Droitwich will see you again before you go."

"Of course," said Tony.

Ma Price shook her head—a head on which, like the Mona Lisa's, all the sorrows of the world seemed to have fallen.

"He hasn't any love left for me—none at all."

"Nonsense!" It was Sir Herbert who spoke. "Of course he has. Now, run along, there's a good woman . . . Tell me, you've been getting your pension all right, haven't you?"

"Oh, yes, I've been getting my pension. But sometimes, I wonder if it's worth it. It seems

like sellin' your birthright for a mess of por-
ridge."

With a final sniff, she permitted Polly to lead
her from the room. Slingsby brought up the
rear of the procession, his manner a nice blend
of disclaiming any connection with the scene
and of apology for having such a sister.

Tony was staring after her.

"What on earth was she talking about?"

"Nothing. Nothing." Sir Herbert flicked his
head irritably, as if shaking off a fly. "She's
tight. Better take her up to your sitting room,
Lydia, and keep her there till it's time for her
to go home."

"Yes, I think you're right."

Tony looked from one to the other in astonishment.

"Good heavens!" he said. "Why? What's all
the trouble?"

"She's a garrulous old fool," said Sir Herbert
shortly, "and in her present condition goodness
knows what she might say to the servants."

"What could she say?"

"Oh, I don't know." Sir Herbert shuffled uncomfortably. "She's quite capable of inventing
stories about your father."

"Why my father?"

"Or me. Or anyone. For heaven's sake, don't keep asking questions."

Tony could make nothing of this.

"What on earth are you so nervous about?"

"Nervous? Nonsense. I'm not nervous."

Tony uttered a sudden whoop.

"My God! I've got it, Uncle Herbert. Ma Price is a bit of your murky past."

"Don't be idiotic, Tony," said Lady Lydia.

"Do *hurry,* Lydia," said Sir Herbert. "Don't stand here wasting time. Get her and keep her with you till she's slept it off. Even now she may be talking."

As the door closed behind Lady Lydia, Tony turned jovially to his uncle, prepared to plumb this thing to the bottom.

"Now, then, Uncle Herbert, look me in the eye. *Was* the good lady anything to you twenty-five years ago?"

Sir Herbert snorted.

"Of course not. Twenty-five years ago I was a hell of a fellow with the pick of the musical comedy field."

"H'm!" said Tony. "Do I believe you or don't I? Your manner is evasive and suspicious. I always wondered why you insisted on Ma Price having a pension."

"Good God, boy! Isn't a faithful servant entitled to a pension?"

"Oh, I don't grudge it her. I'm very fond of Ma—especially at a distance. Of Syd, her offspring, not quite so fond. I suspect that lad of saying nasty things about the aristocracy in Hyde Park. He looks at me with an accusing eye, as if he thought it was me and the likes of me wot block the wheels of Progress. He'd be less severe if he knew what a dashed sweat it was being an earl. I wish *he* could be one for a bit."

"Good God!" Sir Herbert's cry was almost a yelp. "Don't say that."

"Yes, I mean it. I'm fed to the collar stud with all these fellows who think an earl hasn't a care in the world. I suppose they think an estate runs itself. If Syd Price were suddenly to find himself in my shoes . . ."

"Please! Please!"

"What's the matter? What are you quivering about?"

"I'm not quivering."

"You're quivering like some beautiful flower

in a high wind, Uncle Herbert, and what I want to know . . ."

"Oh, 'ere you are!"

The head of Ma Price had insinuated itself round the corner of the door. Sir Herbert Bassinger stared at it as if it had belonged to Medusa.

"Good Lord!" he groaned. "What *is* the matter with Lydia?"

Chapter Five

MA PRICE wriggled coyly into the room. There was a half-emptied glass of port in her hand, and to this was to be attributed, no doubt, the fact that her mood had undergone a very striking change. Whether for the better or not, a critic might have found some difficulty in saying. From the depths of gloom she had soared now to a genial, even an exuberant cheerfulness.

"May I come in? You *are* in." She chuckled amiably. "Well, dearie," she proceeded, beaming upon Lord Droitwich, "now we can have our little chat."

Tony backed a pace. Her footwork was erratic, but she was plainly endeavouring to manœuvre herself into position for a kiss.

"Please, Nannie," he begged, "not now. I'm engaged."

Ma Price chuckled.

"I know you are, dearie. Everyone's talkin' about it. And very 'appy I 'ope you'll be. Three good old cheers—hic!" She paused and looked reproachfully at Sir Herbert. "Oh, Sir Rerbert! I'm surprised."

"What the devil did I do?" demanded that harassed man.

"Why, you . . . hic! That's what you did."

"You'd better come and lie down, Mrs. Price," said Sir Herbert.

The words, for some odd reason, seemed to touch the intruder's womanly pride. She drew herself up haughtily, and her cheerfulness suffered a momentary eclipse.

"No, I'm all ri'," she said with dignity. "Go away. I've been subservient to your orders long enough, Sir Rerbert Bassinger."

"Now, look here, Mrs. Price, I'm not going to stand any nonsense." He wheeled round to the door, through which Lady Lydia was hurrying. "Why the devil did you let her go, Lydia?"

"I never got her," explained his wife simply. "When I reached the pantry, she had disappeared. Apparently, she's been wandering about the house all the afternoon."

Polly Brown appeared in the doorway.

"Oh, you've found her?" said Polly.

Tony looked about him, bewildered.

"Are we playing hide-and-seek?" he demanded.

Ma Price's amiability, ruffled by her late encounter with Sir Herbert, had now become completely restored. She finished her glass of port, and included the entire company in the sunniest of smiles.

"Gents all, and Ladies," she said, resting a hand on a convenient table, "I 'ave a few brief words to say. Now we're all 'ere together, let's drink to this dear boy and his future bride. May all their troubles be little ones! Hic!" She drew herself up rebukingly. "Oh, Lady Lidgier, you *too!*"

Lady Lydia's comment was brief.

"Disgusting woman!" she said.

Once again geniality forsook Mrs. Price. There was a return of the lachrymose mood of what might be described as the First Phase.

"Disgusting, am I?" She pointed a trembling finger at Tony. "Are you going to let them talk

like that to me? I'm fair sick of it, I am. I've
a good mind to tell the whole thing and get it
off me conscience."

Sir Herbert cast an agonized glance at Lady
Lydia.

"Now, listen to me," he said, addressing Mrs.
Price sternly, as if the look had refreshed and
invigorated him. "I want no more of this nonsense. You come in the library and lie down."

Ma Price recoiled from his polluting touch.

"Don't you go laying your 'ands on me!" she
cried shrilly. "It's you that's made me go on
year after year stiflin' the voice of conscience an'
takin' money for it. Go away from me!"

Polly stepped forward.

"I'll take her," she said quietly. "Come along,
Mrs. Price. There's a comfortable sofa in the
library, and I'll fix your hair and make you look
nice for supper."

"You're a good girl, Polly," moaned her
stricken charge, as she allowed herself to be led
away. "Never shot anyone in your life, and so
I told Syd." The name seemed to stir the ancient
fire once more. She turned on Sir Herbert.
"Poor Syd! When I think of the wrong I done
that pore boy, and 'im so kind to me, too . . .

Yes, Sir Rerbert Bassinger, if it hadn't been for you . . . Hic!"

"That will be all, Mrs. Price."

"Will it?" Ma Price seemed doubtful. "Hic! There you're wrong, you see. Anyway, if I 'ave got the hiccoughs, I musta caught them from you."

On this Parthian shot she vanished, brushing past Freddie in the doorway. Freddie, who had come to the drawing room because it had seemed to him that it was getting on for the time when cocktails might be expected to make their appearance, stared after her, frowning.

"Unless my trained eye deceives me," said Freddie, "that woman is sozzled."

"Of course she's sozzled," said Sir Herbert irritably.

"Why don't you turn her over to her foul son and tell him to take her away?"

Lady Lydia uttered a sharp cry.

"She mustn't go *near* her son!"

"Here, what *is* all this?" asked Freddie, perplexed.

Tony came forward. His face was grim.

"That's what *I* want to know," he said. "There's a mystery here."

"No, no, no," said Sir Herbert testily.

"There is. Think I'm a fool? What was all that she was saying about conscience money?"

"Herbert!" Lady Lydia had sunk into a chair. She looked like a woman who has given up the struggle. "Herbert, he's got to know."

"Lydia!"

"Yes, he has. And Freddie, too. I can't stand it any longer."

"Yes, let's have a few explanatory footnotes," said Freddie. "I'm beginning to feel like the hero of an Edgar Wallace novel—wondering which of you is the Strangling Terror and which the Green-Eyed What-Not."

"The old fool is safe enough when she's sober," said Sir Herbert, "but in this state I'm afraid of her."

"Why anyone should be afraid of a nurse once they're grown up, I don't know," said Freddie.

"Tell them, Herbert," said Lady Lydia.

"Yes," said Tony. "I'm waiting, Uncle Herbert."

"Oh, very well," said Sir Herbert Bassinger.

Chapter Six

He went to the door, opened it, and looked
out. He went to the French windows and looked
out of those. Freddie regarded these melodramatic manœuvres with the eye of derision
and seemed about to comment adversely upon
them when Sir Herbert, satisfied that the meeting was tiled, took up his stand in the im-
memorial attitude of English gentlemen—in
front of the fireplace with his hands behind him
—and spoke.

"Tony," he said, "what do you know of the
circumstances of your birth?"

Tony frowned. He was puzzled, and he hated
being puzzled.

"I was born in India . . ."

". . . Where the parents of our hero," added
Freddie, "were stationed at the time. Being a

delicate infant, he was sent back to England in charge of an ayah. . . ."

"Wrong," said Sir Herbert. "Tony was not born in India."

"Then," said Freddie, "the family archives have pulled my leg."

Lady Lydia looked up from her chair.

"Tell him, Herbert," she said.

Sir Herbert Bassinger gulped wryly, like a man swallowing an unpleasant medicine.

"Very well," he said. "Tony, you were born over a barber-shop in Mott Street, Knights-bridge."

Tony blinked.

"What! But how did my mother . . . ?"

"If by your mother," said Sir Herbert, "you mean the late Lady Droitwich, she had nothing to do with it."

The Hon. Freddie Chalk-Marshall could stand just so much. This, in his opinion, was excessive. He regarded the speaker sternly.

"Uncle Herbert," he said, "you've been having a couple!"

"*Tell* him," said Lady Lydia. "Stop beating about the bush."

Sir Herbert explained that he was trying to break it gently.

"Well, don't," said Lady Lydia.

"No," agreed Tony. "Explode your bomb and bury my fragments."

Again Sir Herbert seemed to swallow that unpleasant medicine. He gulped unhappily. Then he braced himself with a strong effort.

"Very well," he said. "This old woman– Mrs. Price—is your mother!"

"My God! You mean . . . ?"

"No. You're not illegitimate. It's worse than that."

"Worse? How could anything be worse? If I were illegitimate, I'd have no right to the title."

"You have no right to the title," said Lady Lydia.

"Are you both mad?"

Sir Herbert uttered a groan.

"It's simple enough, curse it. The Droitwich baby was sent back from India and placed with a wet-nurse. Naturally the woman had to have a child of practically the same age as the other infant."

"Oh, my God!" Tony passed a feverish hand

through his hair. "I see what you mean. The Droitwich baby died, and I . . ."

"The Droitwich baby did not die. He is alive to-day."

"Alive? Where?"

"Outside in the Servants' Hall," said Sir Herbert. "He is Syd Price, the barber."

Into the silence which followed this revelation, there cut sharply an almost animal cry of agony. It did not proceed from Tony, who was staring dumbly at Sir Herbert. This wail of exceeding bitterness came from the Hon. Freddie.

"Syd Price my brother?" cried Freddie, appalled.

"It isn't true," said Tony dully. "It can't be."

"It is, Tony, I'm afraid. Quite true," said Lady Lydia.

Freddie was still wrestling with his private trouble.

"But he *can't* be my brother!" he moaned. "He wears a made-up tie."

Tony walked to the window, looked out, and came back to the group. He sat on the sofa. His face was white.

"I think you had better explain," he said. "Are you sure of this?"

"Quite sure."

"How long have you known?"

"Since you were sixteen."

Tony's eyebrows shot up.

"Twelve years! You've kept it pretty close. How did you happen to find out the truth at just that particular time?"

"That part of it is perfectly simple. There was an accident on one of the suburban railway lines then, and Mrs. Price happened to be in it. She was quite unhurt, but the shock gave her some sort of a heart attack."

"She thought she was dying," explained Lady Lydia.

"And sent for Droitwich," proceeded Sir Herbert. "To tell him the story. In a fit of remorse, you understand. Deathbed repentance sort of thing."

"I see," said Tony.

"I was in my club when he rang me up and asked me to come straight to Knightsbridge. He was very agitated, but he wouldn't tell me anything over the wire . . . said it wasn't safe. So I popped in a cab and went off to this barber-shop, and there Droitwich made Nurse Price repeat her story. . . . The upshot of it was that some time during the year and a half before Droitwich and his wife returned from India she had substituted her baby for theirs."

"I see," said Tony.

Freddie was still struggling gamely against his doom.

"But, dash it, you can't do that sort of thing, you know," he protested. "Wasn't there any family resemblance?"

"I believe the child *was* supposed to look like his father. But, then," said Sir Herbert, "all newly born babies looked like Droitwich."

"You know the type," said Lady Lydia. "Round and pink and vague."

Freddie's hat was still in the ring.

"But weren't there any *marks* on these beastly babies?" he wailed. "There must have been marks. Everybody has marks. You see it in passports—'Any marks?'"

Sir Herbert nodded gravely.

"I'm coming to that. It was that that made the thing a certainty. The Droitwich child had been badly scalded on the arm before it left India. When its parents returned a year and a

half later the scar had disappeared. Nurse
Price explained that it had vanished gradually.
Fourteen years later the boy who is called Syd
Price still bore that scar."

"Then, hang it all," said Tony, "if you were
both satisfied that he was . . ."

"Wait," said Lady Lydia. "He's coming to
that."

"Lady Droitwich," said Sir Herbert, "was in
a very delicate state of health just then. If we
had snatched the boy she thought her son away
from her—the boy she idolized—and tried to
substitute this dreadful little outsider, the shock
would have killed her. All one night Droitwich
and I debated what to do. Then an idea occurred
to me. Supposing we brought the boy to see her
—left him alone with her? Surely the mother
instinct would assert itself . . . ? Surely she
would feel a bond . . . ?"

"And did she?"

"From the moment she set eyes on him," said
Sir Herbert solemnly, "she declared he was the
most impossible little bounder she had ever
seen."

"Couldn't endure him," said Lady Lydia.

"And when her husband tried to suggest **that**

they adopt the lad, she immediately suspected a left-handed relationship. I believe she made things quite uncomfortable for poor Droitwich about it."

Sir Herbert Bassinger drew a deep breath and passed a finger round his collar. He seemed glad to have reached the end of his tale.

"Is that all?" asked Tony.

"Yes—that's all."

"And about enough!" said Freddie.

"I advised Droitwich to leave things the way they were. Here, I pointed out, was one boy trained for the position he was to fill . . . well educated, good manners . . ."

"You've got charming manners, Tony," said Lady Lydia.

"And there was the other boy . . . uncouth, uneducated, a damned unpleasant young feller."

"Amen!" said Freddie.

Tony plucked at the sofa feverishly.

"But what on earth am I going to do?" he cried.

"Do?" There was no hesitation about Lady Lydia's reply. "There's only one thing *to* do."

"Exactly," chimed in Sir Herbert. "Sit tight

and take jolly good care that that old woman keeps her mouth shut."

"But, dash it!" Tony stared. "I can't . . ."

Freddie came across to him and, having patted his shoulder with a kindly hand, gave him the benefit of his mellow wisdom.

"Don't be an ass, old boy," said Freddie rebukingly. "If ever there was a time for not behaving like a silly juggins, this is it. Pull yourself together, laddie. Even if you want to change places with Syd Price, give a thought to *me*. Are you deliberately proposing to land me with a brother like that?"

"Really, Tony," said Lady Lydia, "if the boy's own father didn't think it advisable to set things right, I don't see why *you* should worry yourself."

"Spoken like a man, Aunt Lydia," said Freddie approvingly.

"Worry myself?" Tony turned to Sir Herbert. "Well . . . didn't *you* ever worry yourself?"

"Never! I do all I can for the young fellow. He cuts my hair twice a month when I'm in London."

"And I recommend him to all my friends,"

said Lady Lydia. "That's why he's been able to set up a Ladies' Department."

"And if he hadn't a Ladies' Department," Freddie pointed out, "he would never have met that dashed pretty girl he brought down here to-day. Why, we've done the feller proud!"

Tony gave a short laugh.

"Oh, nobody could criticize your selfless altruism," he said, "but, all the same . . ."

He broke off. Somebody had knocked on the door. A silence fell upon the room. The Family Council exchanged glances.

"Come in," called Tony.

Polly Brown entered. And, as she appeared, a noiseless sigh of relief proceeded from at least three of those present. Lady Lydia expressed hers by smiling pleasantly at the girl.

Polly was composed and calm.

"May I speak to you for a moment, Lady Lydia?"

"Of course. What is it?"

"The thing I would like to ask, if you don't mind telling me," said Polly, "is whether there's any truth in this story of Mrs. Price's."

Chapter Seven

A STUNNED silence followed this devastating question. It was broken simultaneously by Sir Herbert and Lady Lydia. Sir Herbert made an odd, strangled noise like a sheep choking over a blade of grass. Lady Lydia found words.

"What story?" she asked, clenching her hands and gallantly repressing the scream she would have liked to utter.

"About her changing the babies."

"So she's told you?" said Tony unemotionally.

"Yes."

"Confound the woman!" burst out Sir Herbert. "What right has she got, babbling her nonsense to you?"

"I think it was just because I happened to be there," said Polly. "I guess she would have told 'most anybody. And she knows I like Mr. Price."

"You *like* him?" said Freddie incredulously.

"Yes. I'm just mentioning that so you won't think I'm being fresh. I do like Mr. Price. He has always been swell to me, ever since I started working in his shop. And, believe me, it isn't everybody in his line of business who treats girls right when they're working for them. Mr. Price has always been fine to me and that's why I want him to be happy."

Sir Herbert puffed.

"That's all very well, my good girl, but you can't expect Lord Droitwich . . ."

"And that's why," proceeded Polly, "if there *is* any truth in the story, I'd like to ask as a favour that you don't tell it to Mr. Price."

"What!"

"Don't tell it to Mr. Price?"

"Did you say *don't* tell it to Mr. Price?" cried Freddie, tottering. "Was the word you used *'don't'?*"

Polly went on composedly.

"Mr. Price is one of the happiest men you could want to see. He's crazy about his work, and tickled to death because he's making so good. You should hear him talk about how some day he's going to move to Bond Street and that. It's like a kid planning a party. I tell you, he's just suited right where he is. His whole heart and soul are in his business, and he'd be miserable without it. It would spoil his whole life if you suddenly wished a title and a great place like this on him."

"Well!" It was Lady Lydia who first recovered sufficient breath to comment on this aspect of the case. "That's certainly one way of looking at it."

"The only way," said Freddie stoutly. He beamed upon Polly. He approved of her. "I don't know if you realize it," he said, "but every word that falls from your lips is an orient pearl of purest ray serene."

"I'm just trying to look at the sensible side of it. Nobody's going to be happy in this world if they're not comfortable. A king wouldn't be happy if his shoes pinched him."

"Solomon," Sir Herbert assured the company, speaking in a tone of reverence, "was a fool to this girl."

"Mr. Price wouldn't have an easy moment if you made him an earl. He'd always be worrying himself stiff for fear he was going to make a break of some kind."

"She means," interpreted Freddie, who had a smattering of American, "drop some species of brick—perpetrate a floater of sorts."

"He would think folks were laughing at him. And he hates being laughed at. I know," said Polly reflectively, "because I've tried."

Tony was the only person present who did not appear to think that all things were working together for the best.

"Yes," he said, "I daresay you're right. But it's not going to be so jolly comfortable for *me* —living on money that belongs to someone else and hearing myself called Lord Droitwich when I know I'm nothing but an impostor."

Freddie shook his head reprovingly.

"Morbid, old boy. Morbid. Correct this tendency."

"At any rate," said Lady Lydia, "I should think you would find it considerably pleasanter than living in Mott Street, Knightsbridge, and hearing yourself called Mr. Price."

"There's something in that, I suppose."

"And then, of course, there is Violet to be thought of."

"Yes," said Sir Herbert, "you don't want to lose Violet."

"What do you mean, lose her?" demanded Lady Lydia tartly. "The title means nothing to Violet. She told me so."

"Quite," said Sir Herbert hurriedly. "Quite. A fine, unselfish girl."

"Then don't you think," said Polly, "that when a girl is so fine and unselfish as that, it's unfair to take advantage of her?"

"Very well put," agreed Sir Herbert.

He looked anxiously at Tony. So did Lady Lydia. So, with even more intensity, did Freddie. His decision meant a great deal to Freddie.

"All right," said Tony listlessly. "What do a few conscientious scruples amount to between friends? We'll leave things as they are."

"Hurray!" said Freddie.

"Thank heaven!" said Lady Lydia.

"And thank heaven," said Sir Herbert devoutly, "that that intoxicated old fool is safely asleep in the library, where she can't go babbling to anybody. Just fancy if she were dodging about the house, telling that story to everybody she met!"

"I beg your pardon, m'lord," said Slingsby in the doorway, "but could your lordship inform me of the whereabouts of Price?"

Sir Herbert leaped like a harpooned whale. He goggled dumbly.

"What!" he ejaculated, finding speech.

"Don't tell me she isn't in the library!" whispered Lady Lydia hoarsely.

"The library is empty, m'lady."

Polly uttered a cry.

"She must have been playing foxy and pretending to be asleep! Just to get me out of the way. Oh, why was I so easy? I'll never forgive myself—never."

She started for the door. Sir Herbert held up a restraining hand.

"Wait a moment."

"Yes," said Freddie. "We'll need you in this crisis, Slingsby!"

"Sir?"

"Find that young blister Price and send him here."

"Very good, sir."

"Now, then," said Freddie, as the door closed. "If she *has* told the Price excrescence, there's only one hope." He waved his hand toward

Polly. "Kid Solomon, the girl with the bulging forehead."

"Yes," agreed Lady Lydia. "If you can outline your argument as you did to us, you can convince young Price as you convinced Lord Droitwich."

"Aren't you forgetting that it was to Lord Droitwich's advantage to be convinced?" demurred Polly.

"Yes, yes, yes," said Sir Herbert. "But surely if you tell him the job's too big for him to tackle . . ."

"I wouldn't ever say that to Mr. Price. Tell him he can't do a thing, and it puts his back up at once."

"Unpleasant feller!" said Freddie. "I always said so."

Lady Lydia spoke pleadingly.

"But if twelve years ago the late Lord Droitwich himself despaired of turning this young man into a fitting heir to the earldom, ask him what sort of a peer he thinks he would make to-day."

"I know what his answer would be to that."

"What?"

"He'd admit he'd be a pretty queer one, but not any queerer than some of the others."

"He'd be right there," said Tony.

"Well, anyway," said Polly, "I'll go and see what's happening."

"Do," said Sir Herbert. "Yes, do, most certainly."

"And believe me," said Tony, as he opened the door for her, "I'm very grateful for all the trouble you're taking."

Polly smiled at him and went out. Tony shut the door and resumed his place in the Council.

"Now, listen, everybody," said Sir Herbert, in his capacity of self-elected chairman. "I think the wisest course when this young man arrives would be to tackle him at once and offer him money."

"Yes," said Lady Lydia, seconding the motion. "Quite a lot of money."

"A liberal settlement," said Sir Herbert, "on the strict condition that he signs away his claim."

"That's right," said Freddie. "And, mark you, make the offer nonchalantly, as it were."

"I see what you mean." Sir Herbert nodded.

"I understand. As if we were pooh-poohing the whole thing."

"That's it." There was enthusiasm in Lady Lydia's voice. "Highly incredulous and rather amused."

Tony struck a jarring note in this chorus of joy.

"Oh, damn all this plotting and scheming!" he said.

Freddie was obliged once more to rebuke his senior.

"My dear old bird," he said, "there are moments in this life when the only thing is to plot—and to plot like billy-o. You may thank your stars I got my half-blue for scheming at Oxford."

"Oh, all right. I suppose it's necessary."

"It's vital."

"I feel rotten."

"You look great. Now then, all. Practise pooh-poohing. Get ready to be incredulous and amused."

A knock had sounded on the door. The Council became rigid.

"Come in."

Charles, the footman, entered.

"Beg pardon, m'lord," said Charles. "You told me to remind you to dress early to-night."

The Council relaxed.

"Oh, yes. Thank you, Charles."

"Oh, Charles," said Sir Herbert.

"Yes, Sir Herbert?"

"Do you happen to know where young Price is?"

"In the housekeeper's room, Sir Herbert," said Charles. "Talking to his mother."

Chapter Eight

IT IS not often given to a footman to electrify his employer's family as if he had touched off a bomb under their noses. The duties of the junior servants in English country houses seldom afford scope for such a feat. In the whole of England that day, Charles was probably the only youth of his rank who with a single speech had caused a baronet to bite his tongue, a baronet's lady to come within an ace of heart failure, and the second son of an earl to drop his monocle—all simultaneously. And the ironic part of it was that the record breaker had no notion of the sensational deed he had performed; for, after the first involuntary reaction, the members of the Council had recovered their British poise and were themselves again.

"To his mother?" said Lady Lydia. No one

would have guessed from her steady voice that black despair was racking her soul. "Are you sure?"

"Yes, m'lady."

Freddie was even more casual. He had recovered his monocle, and with it the well bred calm of the Chalk-Marshalls.

"How was she, Charles? How *was* the—poor old thing?"

"I fancy she had a notion she was dying, Master Frederick."

An "Oh, my God!" nearly escaped from Sir Herbert's lips, but he choked it back. Nevertheless, a sort of sound, rather like the cry of a mouse in distress, did proceed from him, and Footman Charles attributed it to an aristocrat's kindly concern for a faithful old family retainer. Charles thought it did him credit, and he hastened to reassure him.

"Oh, she'll be all right, Sir Herbert," said Charles, with indulgent respect. "I know her. Inside half an hour she'll be going around singing and laughing."

"Yes, *she* will," said Freddie, with gloom.

"Listen, Charles," said Tony. "Will you ask young Syd Price to come here at once?"

"Very good, m'lord."

The footman retired.

"What's keeping the feller?" demanded Sir Herbert testily. He was still quivering from the shock. "Every dashed person who leaves this room goes off with instructions to find young Price and send him here—and he doesn't come. He doesn't *come,* dash it!"

"Probably finding the old woman's conversation too enthralling. Can't tear himself away," said Freddie.

"This is appalling!" cried Lady Lydia. "She must have told him."

Freddie calmed her with a gesture.

"If she has," he said, "our policy still remains the same. 'Nonchalant' is the watchword. At all costs, let us be nonchalant and even casual. Dash it, if there's any value in education at all, we ought to be able to out-bluff a mere barber."

Sir Herbert mused.

"I shall say . . ."

"Casually," urged Freddie.

"I shall say . . ."

"Nonchalantly."

"Of course, casually. Most certainly nonchalantly. I shall say casually that a rather wild story has been brought to my attention—a story obviously emanating from his mother . . ."

"That's right," said Freddie. "Use long words. Awe him!"

"I will if I can think of some," said Sir Herbert.

" 'Supererogation' 's a good one, if you can work it in," said Freddie helpfully.

There was a sound of footsteps outside the door. Once more the Council stiffened for their ordeal. The handle turned, and Mr. Waddington hurried in, followed by his daughter Violet.

"Lord Droitwich!" cried Mr. Waddington.

"Excuse Father's emotion," said Violet. "The latest Society bombshell has made him all of a twitter."

Sir Herbert stared, aghast.

"Bombshell?"

"Do you mean she's told *you?*" cried Tony.

"She certainly has," said Mr. Waddington.

"What on earth did she want to tell *you* for?" said Freddie peevishly.

"Eh?"

Lady Lydia intervened. She suspected a confusion of ideas.

"Wait a minute, Freddie."

"Well, what business is it of his?" demanded Tony.

"I like that!" said Mr. Waddington, open-mouthed.

"I'm sorry," said Tony. "I was rude. But this thing has made me jumpy. When a man's in danger of losing his title and every penny he has in the world——"

"What in heaven's name are you talking about?" asked Mr. Waddington.

"Didn't you say the old woman had told you?"

"Old woman?"

"Mr. Waddington is talking about your engagement," cried Lady Lydia, in agony. "Your *engagement.*"

Tony stopped.

"My engagement? Good Lord! I was forgetting."

"All very funny and droll," said Freddie, digging up a careless laugh. "Misunderstanding. Two blokes talking on two distinct subjects."

"But what did you mean about losing your title?"

"Nothing, nothing," said Sir Herbert. "Just a joke."

"The purest persiflage," said Freddie.

Mr. Waddington had not made a great fortune in business without possessing a certain native shrewdness. He prided himself on his ability to see through a brick wall as far as the next man. There was something fishy here, he told himself, and he intended to get to the bottom of it.

"It couldn't have been a joke," he said suspiciously. "There's something up. I can tell it by your faces. I can tell it by the way you're behaving, let alone what you've been saying. And I insist on knowing what it is. Now that my little girl has placed her happiness in your hands, Lord Droitwich, I think . . ."

"Yes," agreed Violet languidly. "While I don't often feel the same as Father, *I* think, too . . ."

Tony turned on them viciously. His normal good-nature had not been proof against the happenings of this afternoon. He was in the mood when men crave to smash things. Samson in the Temple felt the same.

"Very well," he said, "if you must have it.

It seems, Mr. Waddington, that I am not really Lord Droitwich."

"Not . . . Lord . . . Droitwich!"

"No. I was changed as a baby."

Violet's shapely eyebrows rose. They had been carefully plucked by an artist of the tweezers, but there was still enough of them left for her to register astonishment.

"Changed as a baby? What do you mean?"

"Well, it's like the story of the 'Baby's Vengeance' in the *Bab Ballads*." Mr. Waddington looked blank. "Never read it? Well, there were two babies, the right one and the wrong one. I'm the wrong one."

"You're the wrong one?"

"Yes. Have you got that? Well, we are now waiting to interview the right one—and—are hoping for the best."

"We think," said Lady Lydia, "we may be able to persuade the other young man to abandon his claim."

"Has he got a case?"

"Oh, yes, he's got a case," said Tony.

"What Father means," said Violet, "is, it isn't like that Tichborne business, where the claimant will blow up under cross-examination? There really is something in it?"

"There is a great deal in it," said Tony grimly.

Mr. Waddington's thumbs shot into the arm-holes of his waistcoat. He waggled the garment belligerently.

"Oh?" he said. "And if he doesn't abandon his claim? How about if he doesn't? Hey? Answer me that. What will you be then?"

"In that case," said Tony, "I shall be a barber."

"If this *is* a joke . . ."

"I told you it was," said Sir Herbert.

Mr. Waddington expressed his feelings in a loud snort.

"No," he said. "I know a joke when I see one."

"A very valuable gift," said Tony.

"And this isn't anything of the kind. It's true. My God! It's *true!* Listen! If this fellow wins his case, do you mean you'll have *nothing?*"

"Not exactly nothing. I shall be the proprietor of a very flourishing barber-shop in Knights-bridge."

"But you'll lose the title . . . and this place . . . and everything?"

"Exactly."

"I think I'm going to have a stroke," said Mr. Waddington.

"Well, don't have it in here," said Freddie. "We're expecting the Claimant at any moment, and a fellow having a fit on the floor would destroy the nonchalant atmosphere. In any case, if you ask me, there are far too many of us here. It'll make him suspicious."

Violet nodded.

"Yes, it *is* a bit of a mob scene, isn't it?" she said. "Come and have your stroke in the library, Father."

Mr. Waddington inhaled deeply and emotionally.

"I'm going to pray," he announced.

"Well, that's all right," said Violet. She turned to Lady Lydia. "He can pray in the library, can't he?"

"He can pray anywhere," replied Lady Lydia wildly, "anywhere!"

"All over the house," said Sir Herbert.

"Thanks most awfully," said Violet.

She shepherded her fermenting parent through the door. As it closed, Tony laughed jarringly.

"And now," he said, "I'm going to get a half sheet of notepaper and make a list of the people in England who don't know all about this secret of ours."

"That's right, old top. Glad to see you perking up," said Freddie. "Good to hear your merry laugh again."

"Merely hysteria," said Tony.

There was a knock at the door. And this time —at long last—it was young Mr. Price in person.

Chapter Nine

SYD PRICE advanced into the room, and Freddie Chalk-Marshall, himself a model of polished calm, eyed his nearest and dearest with silent reproach. The attitude of the Family Council at this terrifically critical moment in their affairs was, in his opinion, all wrong. No good. Rotten. Not a bit like it. With all the emphasis at his command he had urged upon them the vital necessity of being casual and nonchalant. And were they? Not by a jugful. His uncle Herbert was twitching like one afflicted by a sort of gentlemanly palsy. His aunt Lydia looked like Lady Macbeth. And as for his brother Tony—he still preferred to think of him as his brother—a child, and an astigmatic child at that, could have told that he had just received disturbing and distressing news.

A more jumpy, guilty-looking aggregation of blighters the Hon. Freddie had never seen in his puff, and he turned from them with a sigh to inspect Syd.

Well, Syd looked all right, thank goodness. At least, he didn't look all right, because he had always been an ugly sort of Gawd-help-us, and he was an ugly sort of Gawd-help-us now; but what Freddie meant was that Syd looked much as usual. His eye betrayed no sparkle of excitement, such as one might expect to find in the eye of a man who has just been informed that he is the Rightful Earl. His manner appeared to be normal. If he had really been talking to old Ma Price, the latter, Freddie felt, must have confined her conversation to the weather, the crops, and the chances at the next General Election.

So, though his æsthetic objections to Syd remained, Freddie found himself looking at him with pleasure and relief.

"You wished to see me, Sir 'Erbert?" said Syd.

Yes. Voice all right, too. Not a suggestion in it of any lurking triumph and all that sort of thing. Freddie felt that things were looking up, and he lit a cigarette with an air.

Over by the fireplace, Sir Herbert Bassinger was making a perfect ass of himself. Where a curt, crisp inclination of the head or a brisk "Yes" would have been in order, he was wriggling about as if he had got a beetle down his back and positively babbling.

"Quite, quite," said Sir Herbert. "Quite. Exactly. Yes, wanted to see you. We all wanted to see you. . . ."

Here he caught Freddie's eye and subsided guiltily.

"Take a seat " said Freddie, assuming the leadership.

Syd threw him a glance of cold dislike.

"Rather stand," he said curtly.

Freddie felt a little taken aback. Not so good, was his verdict. He had not liked the way the fellow had looked at him.

Lady Lydia entered the conversation. She should not have tried to smile, for the effort was a painful failure, and nothing looks worse at a time like this than one of those smiles that break off in the middle.

"And how is your mother now?" she asked.

Syd did not unbend.

"Nothing the matter with Ma except her imagination. She always thinks she's ill."

"A touch of the sun, perhaps?" said Sir Herbert eagerly. "Thought I had one myself this afternoon."

"A touch of port on top of a flaskful of whisky," replied Syd uncompromisingly. "She's squiffy."

"Dear, dear!" said Sir Herbert. "Now I come to think of it, I did fancy her manner was a little strange when we met. I suppose that in the circumstances—she imagines—imagines——"

"Imagines?"

"Imagines she's ill," concluded Sir Herbert lamely. "Er—Price . . ."

"Yes, Sir Herbert?"

"I—er—wonder—I wonder whether . . ."

"Yes, Sir Herbert?"

"Oh, nothing," said Sir Herbert Bassinger.

He avoided Freddie's eye this time, fortunately for himself. This pitiable exhibition had roused his nephew's scorn to a distressing extent.

Freddie came to the conclusion that it was

time for somebody who was not a gibberer to handle this business.

"Tony, old chap," he said, and his manner was a model of casualness and nonchalance, "didn't you say there was something you wanted to ask Price?"

"Did I?" said Tony feebly.

"Of course." Freddie's eye was now that of an animal trainer. "About his moving to Bond Street."

"Oh, yes," said Tony.

Syd gave Freddie another of those unfriendly looks.

"I'm not moving to Bond Street," he said.

Lady Lydia plunged into the whirlpool again.

"But we think you *ought* to," she said—in Freddie's opinion far too girlishly. "Such a much better class of custom."

"Moving to Bond Street takes capital."

Sir Herbert coughed.

"That's just what we want to talk to you about," he said. "Suppose Lord Droitwich were to give you the capital?"

Syd looked at Tony.

"You, m'lord? Why should you?"

"Well, there *is* a reason," said Lady Lydia.

"Quite, quite," interjected Sir Herbert.

"It's a rather fanciful one, but Lord Droitwich is a fanciful person. He feels that as you were his foster brother . . ."

"Lord Droitwich is always getting hold of some romantic notion. . . ."

"Celebrated for it," said Freddie. "All over Hampshire."

"Well, what do you say. Syd?" asked Tony. "Do you accept?"

Syd looked at him again.

"Accept what? You 'aven't told me your proposition yet."

"Oh, haven't I? Well . . ."

"It's a little hard to put," said Lady Lydia.

Syd transferred his gaze to her. His eye was cold and hard.

"Shall I put it for you?" he said. "You'll give me the money if I sign a paper to say I won't make any claim to being the Earl of Droitwich?"

He surveyed the stunned Council bitterly.

"Yes," he proceeded. "You thought because I came in 'ere and didn't start right off talking sixteen to the dozen that Ma hadn't told me.

Well, she did, see? But I wasn't inclined to take much stock in the story till I come in 'ere and seen how nervous you all were . . ."

"We're *not* nervous!" cried Sir Herbert.

"Oh, you aren't, eh? Well, you jolly well ought to be. Keepin' me out of me lawful 'eritage for twelve years."

Now that she knew the worst, Lady Lydia could be spirited.

"You'll have to prove it *is* your lawful heritage."

"Won't be 'ard to do that. Why, look at that portrait up there." He waved a hand towards the picture of Long-Sword. "Like me as two pins."

"That sort of evidence won't do you much good at the Bar of the House of Lords."

"When I get to the 'Ouse of Lords," retorted Syd, "you won't find me 'angin' about the bar."

"My aunt . . ." began Tony.

"She isn't your aunt," said Syd.

"The lady who has just spoken," emended Tony patiently, "means that you will have to fight your claim."

"Before a special court of me fellow peers. I know that."

Sir Herbert endeavoured to be pompous.

"Now, come," he said. "All this talk is getting us nowhere. Suppose Lord Droitwich . . ."

"He isn't Lord Droitwich."

"Oh, call him X," said Freddie wearily.

"Suppose the family," began Sir Herbert, trying again, "were to settle an income of a thousand pounds a year on you?"

Syd laughed derisively.

"A thousand pounds!"

"It's no use haggling over terms," said Tony. "That's the utmost the estate can stand."

"Good!" Syd chuckled again. "Then I know how much I can offer *you* to clear out quietly and save a lot of expensive lawyer's fees."

Freddie's proud spirit could endure no more of this.

"Of all the bally cheek!" he exclaimed.

Syd turned on him sternly.

"Cheek, eh? Listen. I've 'ad about enough of you. I'm the fifth Earl of Droitwich—get that —and you're my kid brother, see? So don't you forget it. A little more of this and I'll stop your pocket-money."

Freddie gazed up at the ceiling, as if pleading with Heaven to send a thunderbolt. But no thunderbolt came.

"You won't be Lord Droitwich till the courts have declared you so," said Lady Lydia.

"They'll declare me so. Don't you worry— *Auntie!*"

Lady Lydia subsided, stricken to the core. Sir Herbert stepped gallantly into the breach.

"Listen, Price . . ."

"Not so much of your 'Price.' What price *you,* eh? You're goin' to look fine when the *News of the World* gets 'old of this. 'Conspiracy in 'Igh Life. Sharp Sentence on Baronet. Inset —Photo of Sir 'Erbert Bassinger on his way to chokey.' Eh? 'Ow about that?"

"Syd," said Tony quietly.

The Claimant turned to deal with him.

"Yes?" he said. "Let's 'ear from *you.*"

"Have you ever been kicked, Syd?"

The Claimant recoiled.

"None of that, now," he said, alarmed. "None of your 'orseplay 'ere."

"Well, keep a civil tongue in your head, then."

"All right, all right. I can't help it, can I, if I'm bitter and sawcastic and eeronical? 'Oo wouldn't be, situated the way I am? Look 'ere. You're an honest man, I think. Tell me this, straight. Do you believe that by rights I am Lord Droitwich?"

"I do."

"Thank you."

"Don't mention it."

"That's all I wanted to know," said Syd, gratified. "Now I'll go and smoke a cigaroot in the garden and leave you to talk the 'ole thing over quietly." He walked to the table, took a handful of cigarettes from the box, and moved to the French window. "I'll give you ten minutes by my Ingersoll," he said. "Ample."

"Well, that's that," said Tony.

The door opened violently. Mr. Waddington rushed in. He was followed, in her familiar languid manner, by his daughter Violet.

Chapter Ten

"WELL?" cried Mr. Waddington. "Well?"

"Far from it, I'm afraid, Mr. Waddington," said Tony.

"You don't mean . . . ?"

"He knows everything, and is going to fight."

"What," asked Violet, "are the chances of his winning?"

"Extremely good."

"If that infernal old woman gives her evidence," exploded Sir Herbert, "we haven't a leg to stand on."

"My God!" said Mr. Waddington.

"There's just one hope," said Lady Lydia. "We must send for that girl and see what she can do."

"What girl?" asked Violet. "The one he brought down with him?"

"Yes. She may be able to make him see reason. Go and get her, Freddie."

"Right ho."

Violet was raising her eyebrows.

"Why should she make him see reason?"

"She seems to understand him."

"Is she engaged to him, or anything like that?"

"No," said Tony.

"She may be, for all you know," said Violet. "In which case, it seems to me, her interests are all the other way. If our Mr. Price gets the title, she becomes a blushing countess."

"She isn't engaged to him," insisted Tony. "And, from what she said, she wouldn't like to be a countess."

"What an odd girl! Do you think she was dropped on the head as a baby?"

"Now, look here . . ." said Mr. Waddington.

"Oh, shut up!" said Violet.

Mr. Waddington swelled emotionally.

"Oh?" he said. "In my young days, girls spoke respectfully to their fathers."

"They probably had a different kind of father," said Violet.

Freddie returned, bringing Polly. The Council welcomed her effusively.

"Oh, come in, my dear," said Lady Lydia. "We need your advice. Has my nephew told you the situation?"

"In brief outline," said Freddie.

"I understand," said Polly, "Mr. Price knows."

"Yes. So we want you," said Lady Lydia, "to go to him and put the thing as sensibly as you did to us just now."

Polly shook her head.

"It won't do any good."

"What do you mean?"

"If he's been told, then it'll be no use talking to him."

Tony nodded.

"She's right, of course. The only thing we can do is to put up as good a fight as possible."

"Fight to the death!" agreed Freddie approvingly.

"Or don't fight at all," said Polly. "That would be better."

"What do you mean?" demanded Mr. Waddington. "You're talking rot. R-o-t—rot!"

"Don't you believe it," said Freddie. "Here

stands one female who never talks rot. I've been watching her closely, and she's got an idea of some kind. A notion of sorts. A ruse of some description."

"Well, I have," said Polly, "and I think it's a good one. You want Mr. Price not to press his claim, don't you?"

"We do," said Sir Herbert sombrely.

"Well, the only thing that'll make him is if he tries being an earl and finds out how uncomfortable and lonesome and out of place he feels when he is one."

"What on earth do you mean?"

"What I suggest is, let him become Lord Droitwich *now*. *Give* him the old title."

"But, my dear girl . . ." Sir Herbert was disappointed. He had expected better things. "But, my dear girl, we can't give it him. The case has to go before a committee of the House of Lords."

"Yes, but in the meantime you can take him into the house and tell him you're educating him—training him to be Lord Droitwich—fixing him up so's he won't disgrace the family when the case comes on."

Lady Lydia uttered an enthusiastic exclamation.

"What a splendid idea!"

"It *is* an idea," agreed Sir Herbert.

"I told you this girl didn't talk rot," said Freddie.

Mr. Waddington declined to join the chorus of approval.

"I don't see what she's driving at," he grumbled.

"Oh, Father!" Violet had the modern girl's impatience with slowness of wit in her elders. "Use your bean—if any. The idea is to make things so uncomfortable for Mr. Price that he'll throw the thing up of his own accord."

"How?"

"There are a hundred ways," said Sir Herbert. "I'll make him ride."

"I'll take him to *good* classical concerts," said Lady Lydia.

"I'll make his life a misery about clothes," said Freddie.

"Slingsby shall raise his eyebrows and look through him," said Violet.

Freddie pointed out the objection to this suggestion.

"He won't mind that. Slingsby's his uncle."

"Then engage a butler who *can* look through him."

Mr. Waddington had got it at last.

"I see," he said. "It's a splendid idea."

"But not very sporting, what?" said Tony.

"Sporting?" Lady Lydia was shocked. "My dear boy!"

"Well, is it?" insisted Tony. "Pretty low down, it looks to me."

"In a situation as desperate as this," said Sir Herbert, "we cannot afford to be delicate. After all, it's a kindness to the fellow, in a way. Merely showing him what he's up against."

"I see," said Tony drily. "More altruism."

"At any rate, Tony," said Lady Lydia, "you won't be in it. You had better go up to London, out of the way."

"Very well."

"I must be going up to London, too," said Polly. "If Mr. Price is staying here, he won't be able to drive me back."

"I'll take you," said Tony, his gloom lightening for the first time. "Are you all ready?"

"I suppose I had better say good-bye to Mrs. Price."

"All right. I'll meet you at the back entrance in ten minutes."

"Thank you, Lord Droitwich."

"Call me Syd," said Tony.

Lady Lydia turned to Polly.

"Well, Miss Brown," she said, "I can't tell you how grateful we are for your suggestion."

"A pippin," agreed Freddie.

"Thank you, Lady Lydia," said Polly.

A reverent hush followed her departure.

"What a girl!" breathed Sir Herbert devoutly.

"Good brains there," said Freddie. "Solid stuff."

"I don't know when I've seen a girl that impressed me more," said Tony.

Violet looked at him oddly.

"Yes, that was the suggestion you conveyed," she said.

In the slight pause of discomfort which followed this remark, Syd came through the window.

"Now, then," said Syd. He looked suspiciously about him. " 'Ullo! 'Asn't the orchestra bin a bit augmented since I was in here last?"

Tony did the honours.

"My fiancée, Miss Waddington. My fiancée's father, Mr. Waddington. May I present Lord Droitwich?"

Syd seemed a little startled.

" 'Ullo!" he said. "You decided to cave in, then?"

"You put it in a nutshell," said Tony. "I'm going to clear out and leave you in possession." He pulled out a bunch of keys. "This gold master key fits your dressing cases, your dispatch box, your wine cellar, and a few other things which Slingsby will tell you. This is the key to your house in Arlington Street, and this is the key to *this* front door." He threw the ring on the table. "Now, give me the keys to your blasted barbershop, and we'll be set."

Syd stared. Matters were progressing too rapidly for his peace of mind.

"Good-bye, everybody," said Tony. "Good-bye, Aunt Lydia. Good-bye, Uncle Herbert. Toodle-oo, Freddie."

"Tinkerty-tonk, old boy."

"Good-bye, Violet."

"Good-bye, Tony."

Tony turned to Syd.

"Au revoir, Lord Droitwich," he said. "We shall meet at Philippi."

He went out. Syd was looking about him helplessly.

" 'Ere!" said Syd. "What *is* all this?"

He became aware that the company was drifting out.

"Time we were dressing for dinner, Herbert," said Lady Lydia.

"Yes, by gad."

"Coming, Father?" said Violet.

"Eh?" said Mr. Waddington. "Ah? Oh, yes."

Freddie lingered. He was directing at Syd a gloomy eye. Syd met it truculently.

"Well?" said Syd. "A penny for your thoughts."

"I was only thinking," said Freddie, "that, if ever you *should* be called on to take your seat in the House of Lords, I shall make a point of being in the gallery. If there's one thing I enjoy, it's a good laugh."

"Ho!" said Syd.

But he said it to empty space. Freddie had gone. Syd stood for a moment in a reverie; then he moved to the mantelpiece and stared up at the portrait of Long-Sword above it. Somewhat

dubiously he threw himself into the old attitude
—the chin up, the hand on the sword hilt. Then
he moved away again, and presently, as he paced
the room, a new train of thought seemed to strike
him.

He stopped and assumed an oratorical attitude, one hand in his waistcoat, the other flung
spaciously outwards.

"Me Lords!" said Syd, cautiously and in an
undertone. "I rise for the first time in this 'istoric 'ouse . . ."

He broke off in some confusion. Slingsby was
in the room.

" 'Ere!" said the butler, regarding him
morosely.

" 'Ullo, Uncle Ted."

The butler's eye became gloomier than ever.

"Lord Droitwich!" he said scathingly.

"Oh?" Syd, like others had done before him
in that room that day, endeavoured to be casual
and nonchalant. "They bin tellin' you?"

"I know all," said the butler. " 'Urry up, now.
It's time you was dressing for dinner."

"What about clothes?"

"Clothes are being provided."

"Ho!" Syd weighed this information. "Well I want a bath."

"Gawd knows you do!"

"Uncle Ted," said Syd strenuously, "draw me a bath!"

"Draw it your own damn self, m'lord!" replied the butler.

He stalked ponderously from the room. The Droitwich Claimant stood staring after him in silence. In his face there was an expression of growing uneasiness.

Chapter Eleven

IT WAS some two weeks after the sensational events in high life just recorded that Freddie Chalk-Marshall's friend, Tubby Bridgnorth, decided that it was about time he got the old fungoid growth trimmed a bit. Gathering up hat and cane, accordingly, he set out for Price's Hygienic Toilet Saloon. The hour was a few minutes to one. The day was Saturday.

Price's Hygienic Toilet Saloon stands, as has already been mentioned in this chronicle, within a stone's throw of Hyde Park in that little cul-de-sac off the Brompton Road known as Mott Street. It was here that generations of Prices had waged their never-ending war against London's perpetually sprouting hair. It was here that Great-Grandfather Price had once nicked a pimple on a chin no less august than that of the famous Duke of Wellington and had been well cursed for it by that man of plain speech. Most of the nobility and gentry who reside south of the Park came to Price's for their bi-monthly haircuts. Lord Bridgnorth, whose family lived in Cadogan Square, always did.

Holding, therefore, the honourable status of regular client, he was a little piqued on this fine Saturday afternoon to discover that he was not to be attended to, as usually happened, by the proprietor in person. Of Syd, when he entered the shop, there were no signs. The only executive present was a small elderly man with spectacles and a drooping moustache, whose name, though Tubby did not know it and would not have cared if he had, was George Christopher Meech.

Meech draped Tubby in a sheet and got to work on him, and presently the proceedings had reached the stage where the man behind the scissors places a mirror at the back of his patron's head and silently invites him to deliver judgment.

Tubby scrutinized himself narrowly and was not ill pleased. An exacting critic. he found little to cavil at.

"That looks all right," he said.

George Christopher Meech removed the mirror.

"Singe, sir?"

"No, thanks."

"Shampoo, sir?"

"No, thanks."

"Something on the 'ead, sir?"

"No, thanks."

"Very good, sir."

With dignified resignation Meech removed the sheet, and Tubby emerged like some lovely butterfly from its cocoon. He took a closer look at his rubicund reflection.

"Yes," he said. "Not too bad."

"Thank you, sir."

"Of course, you're not the bally artist young Price is."

Meech drew himself up with a good deal of hauteur. He found the remark distasteful. Until two weeks ago he had been employed by the eminent Messrs. Truefitt, whose shop he had left owing to what he was accustomed to refer to guardedly as a misunderstanding; and privately he considered that in coming as far west as the Brompton Road—even to so respected and, in-

deed, historic an establishment as Price's—he
had lowered himself. He resented the suggestion that his technique could be inferior to another's.

"I have not been privileged to witness Mr.
Price's work," he said stiffly.

"He's always cut my hair," explained Tubby.
"And the guv'nor's—when he had any. How do
you mean, you've not seen him at work?"

"Mr. Price has not been on the premises for
a matter of two weeks, sir. I haven't seen him
since the day he engaged me."

"Oh, you're new here?"

"Yes, sir. I used to be in office at Truefitt's,"
said Meech, with the air of one putting somebody in his place.

"And Price hasn't been here for two weeks?"

"No, sir."

"What's become of him?"

"In the country, sir, I understand."

"Oh, taking a holiday?"

A rather mysterious note came into Meech's
voice. He had recovered from his momentary
chagrin and welcomed the opportunity of discussing a matter which had been giving him con-
siderable food for thought.

"If you ask me, sir. I think Mr. Price is re-
tiring."

"What!"

"Yes, sir. I fancy this establishment is coming under new management."

Tubby uttered a startled "Goo' Lord!" He
was astonished. Price's had always been to him
something as stable as the British Museum.
There it was, he meant to say, and there it always had been within the memory of man. He
could remember being brought there by his
nurse to have his curls clipped by the present
proprietor's father. It seemed incredible to him
that the reigning dynasty could ever pass.

"You don't mean Price has sold the place?"

"Whether a sale has actually been consum-
mated, sir," replied Meech in his dignified way,
"I couldn't tell you. But there it is. For two
weeks Mr. Price hasn't set foot in the shop, and
all that while there's been a new man in and
out. Studying conditions, if you ask me, with a
view to purchase."

"What sort of chap?"

"Very nice, well spoken young fellow, sir.
Quite the gentleman. Name of Anthony."

"Oh?" said Tubby.

He was shaken. His was a conservative soul, and he mourned the passing of any London landmark. It seemed sad to him that a shop which had descended from father to son for so many years should pass into the hands of a stranger, nice and well spoken though he might be.

Still, that was the way it went nowadays, mused Tubby sorrowfully. All the old places you had always looked on as fixtures going West on you the moment you took your eye off them. He wouldn't be surprised if at any minute somebody told him that they had pulled down the Cheshire Cheese or Simpson's. Probably they'd abolish the Eton and Harrow match next.

"Well, I hope he's all right," he said. "Because a lot of people have got into the habit of coming here."

He would have spoken further, but at this moment the street door opened, and he perceived the immaculate form of his friend Freddie Chalk-Marshall.

Tubby was surprised. He had imagined that the other was down at Langley End.

"Hullo, Freddie!" he said.

"Hullo, Tubby."

Lord Bridgnorth seemed still to be under the

impression that there was an outside chance of this being a mirage or figment of the imagination.

"Are you in London?" he asked, to settle this point.

Freddie assured him that he was.

"Tony in London?"

"Er—yes," said Freddie. "Yes, Tony's in London."

"The whole blooming family in London?"

"Yes. We moved up from Langley End yesterday."

Freddie spoke like one on his guard, weighing his words. Into his manner, as he gazed at his old schoolmate, there had crept a certain wariness. The last thing Freddie wanted, while the family affairs were in their present delicate state, was a young Gossip Page writer prowling about the danger zone. Up to the present, no whisper had gone abroad of what had occurred at Langley End that fatal summer day; but you never knew when something might not leak out, and unaware that Price's had been a haunt of Tubby's since childhood, he found himself suspecting his motives for being there.

He eyed his friend, accordingly, askance.

Tubby, he reflected, had always been a pretty asinine sort of old ass, but somebody might have tipped him off about this business.

"What brings you here?" he asked.

"Haircut. What have *you* come for?"

"Shave, sir?" inquired Meech professionally.

"I wanted a word with the fellow who runs this place," said Freddie.

Meech could help him here.

"Mr. Anthony was in a short while back, sir —talking to Miss Brown, our manicurist. He stepped out."

"Likely to be long?"

"I fancy not, sir. I think I heard something said about coming back with some lunch and the two of them having it in here together."

Meech sniffed a little as he spoke these words. At Truefitt's, picnic luncheons in the toilet saloon are unknown. If Mr. Truefitt wants a snack, he goes elsewhere for it.

Tubby was interested.

"Have you met this chap, Anthony?"

"Yes," said Freddie. "I've met him."

"How?"

"Oh, just the way you do meet people."

"Where?"

"What does it matter where?"

"What do you want to see him about?"

"Just something. You're dashed inquisitive," said Freddie coldly.

"Merely asked."

"Why?"

"I'm interested in the man."

"Why?"

"Well, dash it," said Tubby, "I've been coming here to have the surplus growth removed ever since I was a kid, and I breeze in to-day, thinking everything's much the same as usual, and this bloke here . . ."

"Meech is the name, sir," said George Christopher helpfully.

"And Mr. Meech here tells me the place has been sold to a mysterious bozo of the name of Anthony. I want to know who he is and all about him, and whether he can be trusted to look after the old thatch the way Price used to."

Freddie's suspicions were not yet lulled.

"You're sure that was really the reason?"

"What do you mean?"

"You didn't come in your journalistic capacity, nosing round for material for your Gossip Page?"

Tubby's mystification increased. His friend seemed to him to be speaking in riddles.

"I don't know what you're drivelling about. What *are* you drivelling about?"

"Oh, well, if you're not, never mind. I thought you might be."

"What?"

"Nosing round for material for your Gossip Page."

"I haven't a Gossip Page now. I've retired."

"They've fired you?" said Freddie, leaping to the natural conclusion. He had often wondered how long a responsible newspaper with a duty to its public would put up with the sort of bilge old Tubby ladled out. "When?"

Young Lord Bridgnorth resented the slur.

"They didn't fire me. They were particularly pleased, as a matter of fact, with the brightness and intelligence of my work."

"Then why have you left?"

"Haven't you heard?"

"Heard what?"

Lord Bridgnorth grasped the lapel of his friend's beautifully form-fitting coat and prepared to deliver the big news.

"I'm engaged!"

"Engaged?"

"Absolutely. To Luella, only daughter of J. Throgmorton Beamish, of New York City."

Freddie was duly impressed.

"You don't say!"

"I do say. I've just *been* saying."

Freddie lighted a cigarette.

"Blind girl?" he asked.

"What do you mean, blind girl?"

"Well, she'd have to be, wouldn't she? However, hearty congrats. When did you pull this off?"

"A couple of days ago. It was in the *Morning Post* yesterday."

"I never read the *Morning Post*. In fact, what with one thing and another . . ."

The Hon. Freddie Chalk-Marshall paused. A sudden idea seemed to have smitten him. His eyes gleamed with the light seen only in the eyes of genuine go-getters.

"This Beamish," he said. "Is he rich?"

"Crawling with the stuff."

"And bald?" asked Freddie keenly.

"Of course he's bald. All Americans are."

"Then what he needs," said Freddie, "is

Price's Derma Vitalis. Marvellous stuff. I gave you a bottle of it once."

"Did you? Oh, yes, I remember now. I broke it."

"Then you were a silly goof and an ass of the first water," said Freddie. "It would have made all the difference to your health and happiness." He turned to Meech. "Send round half a dozen bottles of that hair lotion of Price's to Lord Bridgnorth, Drone's Club, Dover Street."

Meech was pleased. This was big business.

"Very good, sir."

"You can hand them on to the old boy, Tubby."

Lord Bridgnorth seemed dubious.

"But, listen," he said. "I can't go loading old Beamish up with hair tonics. I don't know him well enough."

"You're going to marry his daughter, aren't you?"

"Not if I go loading him up with hair tonics. I've come to the conclusion that it doesn't pay to harp on the subject of baldness with these hairless birds. Look what happened with my old guv'nor."

"Never mind that . . ."

"And for that matter," proceeded Lord Bridgnorth, "look what happened with Elisha."

"Elisha Who?"

"Just Elisha. The chap in the Old Testament. He hadn't a hair on his bean, and when a bevy of children pointed out the fact to him, what ensued? Bingo! Eaten by bears!"

Freddie moved restlessly on his elegantly shod feet. He appreciated the force of his friend's arguments, but the salesman was very strong in him. He mused tensely.

"Look here," he said at length. "When are you seeing the Beamish again?"

"He's lunching with me at the Ritz. We're going to the Tower of London."

"Then take me along and let me make a sales talk."

The idea found favour with Lord Bridgnorth.

"Oh, well, if you spring it on him as your idea . . . I mean to say, if you're the one who'll be attended to by the bears . . . right ho."

Freddie looked at his watch.

"I can just manage a quick lunch. I'm riding in the Row with a fellow at two-thirty."

"What fellow?"

"Just a fellow."

"I bet it's a girl."

"I wish it was," said Freddie. "When Mr. Anthony returns," he said to Meech, "tell him Mr. Chalk-Marshall was looking for him and will be back anon."

"Very good, sir."

Tubby came back to the old theme.

"How well do you know this bird Anthony?"

"Slightly," said Freddie. "Very slightly."

"Who is he?"

"Just a bird," said Freddie. "His name's Anthony. Come on."

He led his friend into Mott Street, where they hailed a taxicab and set out for the Ritz. He congratulated himself on a good morning's work. Shaken to the core though he had been by the recent family upheaval, Freddie Chalk-Marshall had never forgotten that he was a man with a mission.

Chapter Twelve

For some minutes after the departure of the bridegroom-to-be and his salesman friend, Meech (late of Truefitt's) had the shop to himself. He occupied his leisure, as a good barber should, in making things ready for the next rush of custom. He stropped a razor, rearranged divers soaps and unguents on the shelves, straightened one of the advertisements on the wall, told an inquiring child the correct time, and then, feeling that there was little more to be done till the next customer arrived, went to the street door and stood on the threshold, drinking in what passed for air in Mott Street.

Following a train of thought which had been started by the spectacle of a number of purposeful-looking men seeping through the entrance

of the Caterpillar and Jug on the corner, he had
just begun to debate within himself the possibility of slipping in there for a quick one when
the door of the public house opened, this time
to allow a client to emerge.

This client was a massive young man of pleas-
ing appearance, whose progress was hampered
by a number of parcels which he carried. The
sight of him sent Meech hurrying back into the
shop, where he proceeded to strop another
razor, thus showing zeal. And presently there
came from the street outside a musical whistling,
and there entered to him his employer, the well
spoken Mr. Anthony.

"Hullo, Meech," said the new arrival. "Here
I come, whizzing back."

"Glad to see you, sir," said Meech courteously.

"Stropping a razor, I note."

"Yes, sir."

"Strop on, Meech, strop on."

Tony deposited his parcels on a table which
stood beside the door marked "Ladies' Dept."
For a man who had so short a while before
suffered a grievous blow to his position and
prestige, he was looking remarkably cheerful.

No sign of care was on his face. He had the appearance of one who found existence entirely attractive.

Nor would his appearance have misled the observer. Taking it for all in all, Tony had never been happier in his life.

There is much to be said for being a peer of the realm with large estates in the country and a big house in Arlington Street. A man in such a position may be ranked as sitting pretty. But —and it was this discovery which was causing Tony to exhibit such a shining face to the multitude—there is even more to be said for being the proprietor of a Hygienic Toilet Saloon whose staff includes a girl like Polly Brown.

Two weeks is ample time for a young man of ardent temperament to confirm his first, hastily formed suspicion that he has met the only girl he could ever love. At the conclusion of this period Tony's mind had become a mere receptacle in which dwelt the image of what textbooks call the adored one. Seeing Polly daily, being in constant close communion with Polly, he had arrived at a mental condition where very few things in life besides her had any real existence.

George Christopher Meech would have been surprised to hear it, but he figured in his employer's eyes merely as a sort of phantasm.

In Polly, Tony told himself that he had at last discovered the girl of his boyhood dreams. Yet, oddly enough, she was not in the least like the object of those dreams, for, as a boy, his tastes—built, probably, on the vision of the hefty Principal Boy of some early pantomime—had tended towards the stately, the beautiful, and the buxom. But he had only had to see Polly twice before realizing that, emotionally, he had reached Journey's End.

He loved her quaintness, her shrewd philosophy, the brown glow of her face, the sparkle that came so readily into her eyes and was the immediate forerunner of that wonderful smile of hers.

A girl in a million.

He would go farther. Two million. Or three.

Having disposed of the parcels, Tony began to expend some of his effervescent spirits in pleasant conversation. Phantasm though Meech was, he enjoyed talking to him. He found this wraith entertaining.

"How's business been?" he asked.

"Quiet, sir. Very little doing. I cut a gentleman's hair."

"Good."

"But he declined a singe, a shampoo, and any lotion for the scalp."

"Bad."

Meech smiled paternally.

"No need to get discouraged, sir. My experience is that the rush comes of an afternoon on Saturdays."

"Oh? Of an afternoon, eh?"

"Yes, sir. By the way, sir, a Mr. Chalk-Marshall was in here not very long ago, asking for you."

"Oh? So they're up in London. Did he leave any message?"

"Yes, sir. He said he would be returning later."

"Good. And now," said Tony, "will you go and hang the 'Shop Closed' sign on the door."

Meech did not actually reel, but he seemed to come very near to reeling. All the professional in him was shocked.

"You're shutting up the shop, sir?" he gasped.

"I am."

"At one o'clock? Of a Saturday afternoon?"

Tony had been unwrapping his parcels.
These, divested of their coverings, now revealed
themselves as sandwiches. There was also a
gold-leaf-decorated bottle with a couple of
glasses. The bottle had the subtly grim look of
champagne which has been bought at a public
house.

"I suppose it *is* irregular," he said. "But what
would you?"

"Yes, sir," said Meech doubtfully.

"Or, putting it another way," said Tony,
pointing the bottle earnestly at him, to em-
phasize his remarks, "what the hell?"

"Quite, sir," said Meech. He was completely
at a loss, but it seemed a safe thing to say.

Tony developed his argument.

"I am young, Meech. The sun is shining. I
have a lady lunching with me. And I do not wish
to be disturbed. Therefore, I close the shop. To
blazes, Meech, with this modern craving for
wealth. What does it matter if we do let a few
shilling haircuts get past us?"

"Shaves, mostly, sir, on a Saturday."

"Or shaves, either. The hot blood is running
in my veins, Meech, and I'm going to enjoy myself to-day, even if the shop goes bust."

Meech sighed.

"Just as you please, sir. It's your shop."

"That's just what it is."

"And you're running it professionally?"

"Of course."

"I thought you might be one of these young swells doing the thing for a lark."

"Far from it."

"You'll excuse me saying it, sir, but you're what I might call a Man of Mystery. This Mr. Chalk-Marshall was a very high-class young gentleman, and he spoke as if he knew you intimately."

"He does."

"That's what I mean, sir," Meech pointed out triumphantly. "That's what makes me call you a Man of Mystery."

Tony patted him on the shoulder.

"I'm just a young fellow trying to get along," he said. "But don't let's talk about me. Let us discuss Miss Brown. Where *is* Miss Brown?"

"In the Ladies' Department, sir, I fancy. Doing a head of hair."

"Oh? Well, I hope she won't be long. The champagne's getting cold."

"Shall I go and inquire, sir?"

"No, never mind. You run on home and play with the children."

"I am not married yet, sir."

"Not yet?"

"No, sir. But we're beginning to talk about it. We've been engaged now for eight and a half years."

Tony regarded his assistant with frank interest. One of the minor compensations of his changed life was that it had plunged him into the society of people like Meech. He was always learning something new about Meech. Only yesterday he had discovered that he played the saxophone—the very last instrument, somehow, of which anyone would have suspected him.

"You're one of these Marathon lovers," he said.

"It doesn't do to plunge rashly into matrimony, sir."

"I absolutely disagree with you," said Tony warmly. "I am all for the swift, sudden dive."

A tolerant smile flitted across Meech's face—the smile canny middle-age reserves for headstrong youth.

"I used to think that once, sir. That was when I was engaged to my other young lady."

Tony was interested.

"Oh? There was another young lady, was there?"

"Yes, sir," said Meech. He was always glad to confide the story of his life to a sympathetic ear. "But she did the dirty on me and ran away with a postman. . . ."

"No!"

"Yes, sir. Just after her birthday, too."

"Awful!" said Tony. "I'm afraid some women are like that—mercenary and flighty."

"But not all of them, sir," said Meech loyally.

"Meech," said Tony warmly, "you spoke a mouthful."

"My present young lady would never do a thing like that."

"You're sure?"

"Quite sure, sir."

There was a pause. Tony fiddled with shaving soaps.

"By the way, Meech," he said, "tell me something. These two young ladies—how did you approach them—propose to them, I mean?"

"Oh, well, sir . . ."

"No, seriously. I want to know. It's a dashed difficult thing to propose."

"Well, my experience, sir, is that it just 'appens the way it 'appens to come."

Tony appeared to be digesting this pronouncement. He repeated the words thoughtfully.

"It just happens the way . . . Do you know, I don't quite get that."

"What I mean, sir, is that these things depend largely on what you might call the inspiration of the moment."

"Oh? The inspiration of the moment?"

"Yes, sir. You see what looks to you like an opening, and you take it. For instance, with my first young lady we just happened to be sitting in a cemetery, and I asked her how she'd like to see my name on her tombstone."

"And the remark was well received?"

"Oh, very, sir."

"But you didn't stop there?"

"No, sir. I went on from there. That was only the start."

"I see . . . What was your method of approach the second time?"

A Don Juanian glitter appeared behind Meech's spectacles. He seemed to be recalling old, far-off, happy things.

"Well, that was after the movies had come along," he said, "so of course it was different."

"What had the movies got to do with it?"

"They're emotional, sir—full of what you might call emotional stimulus. It stands to reason a girl don't see Ronald Colman for nothing. With my present young lady I just walked up to her and took her in my arms and kissed her."

"And she liked it?"

"She gave every evidence of doing so, sir."

Tony regarded the impetuous man with admiration.

"And you've lived up to that for eight and a half years? I think you're marvellous."

"I haven't heard any complaints, sir," said Meech complacently. "Haven't *you* ever been engaged, sir?"

It was a simple question, but, as he heard it, something like a douche of icy water seemed to strike Tony between the eyes.

"Gosh!" he exclaimed.

In all this magic two weeks, if Tony had given a thought to Violet Waddington, it had been only a passing thought—the kind of mental peck a man gives at something unpleasing that has formed part of a life with which he has fin-

ished. He had regarded Violet as a thing definitely of the past.

And yet . . . had anything been said to indicate that she considered their arrangement
annulled? No, he was forced to admit, nothing
had been said. For all he knew, she looked upon
him still, despite his altered circumstances, as
the man she was going to marry. He might have
taken it for granted that the engagement was
at an end, but there had been nothing to indicate
that she also assumed this. At this very moment,
in short, a girl he was not even mildly fond of
might be going round the dressmakers' shops,
buying the trousseau.

He was appalled. Standing there, he could
not imagine how he had ever come to make such
an ass of himself that summer morning in the
rose garden at Langley End. He looked back
on the scene. She had been about there, he had
been about here . . . a nice, safe three feet or
so between them. Not a sign of danger. And
then . . . suddenly . . .

He writhed, as every smallest detail of the
scene rose up before him. After what had passed
in that rose garden there was no backing out for

him. If she still wished to marry him, he was for it.

"Gosh!" he cried. "I *am!*"

"Indeed, sir?" said Meech, interested. "And how did you meet your young lady?"

"Meech," said Tony, "I didn't meet her. She sort of overtook me."

Once again the assistant found himself at a loss. He gazed upon Tony and found him cryptic. Before he could ask for elucidation, however, the door marked "Ladies' Dept." opened, and Polly appeared.

Polly was looking wonderful. She seemed to bring a breath of springtime into a room which, to a fastidious sense, was too heavily laden with the scent of brilliantine and Tubby Bridgnorth's hair. And at the sight of her Tony's gloom vanished as that hair had vanished beneath the clippers of George Christopher Meech.

If one quality more than another predominated in Tony's spiritual make-up, it was the quality of resilience. You could turn him from an earl into a barber and he would come up smiling. And, similarly, you could saddle him with a girl he disliked, yet the moment the girl he loved came in view, up soared his spirits and he was his care-free self again.

The future, felt Tony buoyantly, could take care of itself. All that mattered was the present. And that present involved a tête-à-tête lunch with Polly Brown.

Tête-à-tête, that is to say, if he could but get rid of the adhesive Meech, whose demeanour suggested that he intended to stay and see this thing through if it took all summer.

"Oh, *there* you are!" said Tony. "I've been waiting hours."

"Five minutes only, sir," said Meech, a stickler for the accurate.

Tony was annoyed with Meech.

"Well, it seemed like hours—talking to you," he said, coldly. "Go and hang the 'Shop Closed' sign on the outer battlements."

"You aren't closing the shop!" cried Polly. "On a Saturday?"

"Just what *I* said to him, miss," observed Meech, with satisfaction.

Tony brandished the bottle of champagne.

"No arguments, please! No back-chat." He suddenly perceived what he was doing. "Gosh!" he said, eyeing the bottle doubtfully. "I oughtn't to be waving this . . . Or ought I? . . . It may make it better." He inspected the label with some distaste. "I've never met this particular brand. I wonder if it will pop. I think you had better watch me, Meech, and, when I open this, make a popping sound with your mouth. It will add what you might call atmosphere. Oh, but I was forgetting. You're just going, aren't you? Well, buzz off."

"If you really are determined to close the shop, sir—at one o'clock—of a Saturday afternoon . . ."

"All right, all right. I know."

"Then there's nothing to keep me."

A sudden gleam came into Tony's eye. He looked at his assistant with the alertness of a Druid High Priest inspecting the human sacrifice.

"Unless you'd like me to shave you first," he said insinuatingly.

"No, sir," said Meech firmly. "No, thank you, sir."

"I've got an itch to shave somebody. What you might call a barber's itch."

"Your luncheon appears to be ready, sir," said Meech, with veiled reproach.

"I don't believe you approve of us lunching on the premises, Meech."

"It is not for me to criticize, sir," said Meech with dignity, "but it would never have done at Truefitt's."

The door closed behind him, and Tony turned to his guest, who was setting out the sandwiches.

Chapter Thirteen

Good chap, Meech," said Tony, as he took his seat at the board, "but a bit of a snob. Never lets you forget he has come down in the world."

Polly was munching a sandwich with the healthy zest of a girl who has earned her luncheon by a morning's work.

"I wonder why he left Truefitt's," she said.

"It's one of those dark secrets so common in hairdressing circles," said Tony. "You hear whispers from time to time in the crack barbers' clubs like the Senior Bay Rum or the Snippers, but nobody knows anything definite."

"Perhaps he was an earl."

Tony considered the point.

"Possibly," he said. "But I don't think so. We ex-earls have a sort of indefinable something about us which it is almost impossible to mistake. I cannot detect it in George Christopher Meech. Personally, I believe his downfall was due to pure chivalry. He accepted dismissal to protect a woman's name."

"What woman?"

Tony ate a sandwich thoughtfully.

"As I see it," he said, "she was a little blue-eyed manicurist—frail but very lovable. Her meagre salary went to support an invalid father. For a time, all was well. Every Saturday she brought home her slim envelope, and they spent the contents on rent and groceries and an ounce of tobacco for the old man. And then one day, returning to their modest flat, she found tragedy awaiting her."

"He wasn't dead?"

"Not dead, but going bald. You can imagine what that meant. Come what might, he had to have hair restorer. And where could she find the money to buy hair restorer? She couldn't. It wasn't possible. All through the Sunday, far into the night, Mabel—her name was Mabel—brooded wretchedly. And then, while eating a kipper at breakfast on the Monday morning, she found the solution. She remembered that Mr. Truefitt kept a bottle of hair restorer on an upper shelf in the room where she and George Christopher Meech had worked side by side for so many months."

Polly trembled.

"She isn't going to steal it?"

"She jolly well is," said Tony firmly. "She stole it that very day when Meech was out to lunch. And a few mornings later Mr. Truefitt sent word that he wished to see Meech in his private office."

Tony took another sandwich and ate for awhile in silence.

"Well, you can guess what had happened. The theft had been discovered. Mr. Truefitt put it squarely up to Meech. Either Meech or Mabel was the guilty person. And Meech was true as steel. He could have proved an alibi, but he preferred to take the blame on himself. 'It was I, Mr. Truefitt,' he said, in a quiet, steady voice. Mr. Truefitt was visibly shaken. 'Think well, George,' he said kindly, for he loved the lad. 'Do you really mean this?' 'I do, sir,' said Meech. There was a long silence. Mr. Truefitt heaved a sigh. 'So be it, George,' he said. 'If that is your story, there is nothing to be done but to let justice take its course.' And that after-

noon all the assistants formed in hollow square,
with Meech in the middle, and Mr. Truefitt
formally stripped him of his scissors."

"What a man!" said Polly reverently.

"Mr. Truefitt? Or Meech?"

"Meech."

"A silent hero," agreed Tony.

He reached for the bottle of champagne.

"Are you ready for a little of the Cuvé
Lucrezie Borgia?"

"Thanks."

"By the way, Freddie was in this morning."

"Did you see him?"

"No. But I believe he's coming back."

"I wonder how they are all getting on."

"Yes. It will be nice to get some news." Tony
gave the bottle a wary look. "You know, I think
we ought to try this stuff on the mice first. It
may be lethal."

"I've never tasted champagne before."

"You certainly aren't going to taste it now,"
said Tony. He pulled the cork, and there was an
encouraging report. "Well, it popped, anyway,"
he said, with satisfaction. He filled the glasses
and pushed one of the paper bags towards her.
"Have a pickle. It may help the flavour."

Polly sipped.

"I think it's good," she said.

Tony sipped.

"It might be worse," he agreed. "It tastes a little like Price's Derma Vitalis."

Polly put her glass down.

"I think you're wonderful," she said simply.

"Me?" Tony, though gratified, was surprised. "Why?"

"It isn't many men who would be so cheerful in your position."

"Lunching with you, do you mean? But I like lunching with you."

"You know what I mean. It must be pretty awful coming down to this—after what you've been."

"Not a bit of it. I've had the time of my life these last two weeks."

"Have you?" said Polly, a little wistfully.

"I'm in my element. My ancestors were all barbers, and in this atmosphere of bay rum and brilliantine my storm-tossed soul finds peace. Blood will tell, you know."

Polly drank her wine in little birdlike sips. Her face was thoughtful.

"Do you really believe you are Mrs. Price's son?" she asked at length.

"I do. Don't you?"

"No. I think she's dippy."

"This is very interesting. Have a sandwich."

"And what's more," went on Polly, "when the time comes, I don't think she'll go through with it."

"No?"

"No. She'll go back on her story."

"What makes you think that?"

"Just a hunch."

"Has she said anything to you about it?"

"Lots. Whenever I meet her. She's full of remorse."

"Poor old thing," said Tony sympathetically. "It must be a rotten position for her. I should think she must feel like someone who has dropped a match in a keg of gunpowder."

Polly flashed a glance of covert approval across the table. Of all the qualities which she found admirable in Man, she ranked highest the ability to be a good loser. Tony seemed to her the best loser she had ever met. Not once since that fateful day had he given so much as a hint of self-pity.

"It can't be very pleasant for anyone," she said. "Sir Herbert, for instance. Or Lady Lydia."

"Or Freddie." Tony chuckled. "Poor old Freddie, how he must be hating it."

"And Slingsby. Fancy having to call your nephew 'Me lord'!"

"A very nasty mess altogether," agreed Tony, "and one that does not bear contemplating. Let's forget it and discuss where you and I are going this afternoon."

"Are we going anywhere?"

"Of course we are. You must spend the afternoon in the open on a fine day like this. I'm a business man, and I figure I'll get more work out of you if you have plenty of fresh air in your lungs."

Polly looked at him oddly.

"You mustn't spoil me," she said. "Remember, *I've* got to go on earning my living after you're an earl again."

"You will have it that I'm going to be an earl again. Personally, I don't feel it. I rather fancy you will find me here forty years from now, working away in the shop in a skullcap and a full set of white whiskers. The lovable old barber, what? I can hear people saying, 'Oh, you must patronize that quaint old blighter. He's quite a character.'"

"Forty years from now, you'll be a gouty old earl, telling everybody the country is going to the dogs."

"You think so?"

"I know it."

Tony nodded indulgently.

"Well, if that's your story, as Mr. Truefitt said to Meech, I suppose you're right to stick to it. Can't see it myself. But we're wandering from the point. Where do we go this afternoon in the old sidecar? The river? Sunny Sussex? Give it a name."

A queer little twisted look came into Polly's face.

"I don't think I'd better go out in the sidecar any more," she said in a small voice.

"Why not?"

"Oh, I don't know."

"Why not, Polly?"

Polly met his eye bravely, though her lips were trembling.

"Well, listen," she said. "When I was a kiddy, I used to be sent out to my grandfather's farm in Connecticut for two weeks every summer. And gee, did I love it! It was like heaven. But one year I refused to go any more. You see, I loved it too much, and I knew how awful it was going to be when it was over."

She broke off and looked away. Across the table Tony gave a gasp. He reached for her hand.

"Polly! . . . Do you mean . . . ? Oh, hell!" said Tony.

He released her hand abruptly. The sound of an opening door and a current of Mott Street air on the back of his head had warned him that they were no longer alone.

Tony turned, annoyed. His first thought was that George Christopher Meech had returned, and it was his intention to speak firmly and bitterly to Mr. Meech. Then he perceived that he had been mistaken. The intruder was Slingsby.

The butler was resplendent in the morning coat and bowler hat in which he took his walks abroad when in the metropolis. He was puffing gently, for the fine weather had tempted him to make the journey from Arlington Street on foot, and his condition was not of the best.

"Hullo!" said Tony.

"Good-afternoon, m'lord."

There was respectful benevolence in Slingsby's eye. A shepherd, inspecting a lost sheep which he had always regarded as a social superior, would have looked the same. The decision of Sir Herbert Bassinger to run up to London for a couple of weeks had met with the butler's unqualified approval. He had had much to endure since Tony's departure from Langley End, and he had longed to see him again and confide his troubles to him.

Observing that a meal was in progress, he dropped with smooth efficiency into his lifelong rôle. Advancing to the table without further words, he picked up the bottle, looked at the label, winced, and poured wine into the glasses. This done, he took up his stand in a professional attitude behind Tony's chair.

"Now, now, Uncle Ted!" said Tony, "you mustn't wait on us."

"I prefer to wait on your lordship."

"I'm not your lordship. I'm your nephew."

"I prefer to regard your lordship as your lordship."

Polly, with womanly tact, solved a difficult *impasse*.

"We've finished," she said. "At least, I have. Have you?"

"Quite finished," said Tony.

Polly rose and began to tidy the table. She did it expertly, gathering up the paper and débris with a minimum of disturbance. She waved away Tony's offer of assistance.

"Sure you can carry all that?"

"Quite, thanks."

"Not too heavy for your frail strength?"

"I'm stronger than I look," said Polly.

She pushed open the "Ladies' Dept." door and went through. Tony got up and lighted a cigarette.

"Nice of you to look in," he said. "I heard the family were up in London. How's everything at home?"

A heavy frown marred the placidity of the butler's face.

"There is only one word for it, m'lord," he replied, sombrely, "Itchabod!"

Tony puffed thoughtfully.

"Itchabod, eh?"

"Yes, m'lord."

"You mean things aren't going well?"

"No, m'lord."

"Well, I don't know what's to be done about it." Tony seated himself on the table. "You see, my dear chap . . ." The butler winced. "You see, my dear chap," Tony went on, ignoring his distress, "we've got to face facts. You know and I know that I'm not Lord Droitwich . . ."

It was not Slingsby's habit to interrupt the Family, but he could not refrain from doing so now.

"I know nothing of the kind, m'lord. I've watched that young Syd, and nobody's going to tell me he's a naristocrat. A man with the blood of noble ancestors in his veins," said Slingsby, warming to his theme, "might possibly use a fish knife for the ontray, but he would never take a piece of bread and mop up his gravy with it."

"Oh, he'll train on. You must give him time."

"I'd give him ten years," said the butler viciously, "if I 'ad my way."

He would have spoken further, but at this moment the Ladies' Dept. door opened again, and through it came a figure which smote the words from his lips.

"Ho!" he said. "You, eh? I want to see *you*."

Ma Price gulped silently. She was a very different woman from the alternately jaunty and lachrymose person who had zigzagged about the ancient interior of Langley End two weeks ago. True, she seemed lachrymose now, but the tears that threatened were not vinous tears. They proceeded from spiritual anguish rather than from alcoholic stimulant. She was all black satin and agony.

Polly, following her through the doorway, saw the butler's portentous figure looming like a thundercloud.

"Please don't be mad at her, Mr. Slingsby," she pleaded. "She's not happy."

Another gulp escaped Ma Price. It was the equivalent of a "Hear, hear!" at a public meeting. She had not passed an enjoyable two weeks. Tony's suggestion that her emotions must be those of one who has touched off a keg of gunpowder was accurate. If anything, it did not go far enough. She felt as if she had punched a hole in a dam and were watching thousands perish in the valley below.

The butler refused to be diverted from his victim.

"And what *right* has she to be happy," he

demanded remorselessly, "the way she's acted?"

Ma Price sniffed miserably.

"I'm sure I never meant no 'arm."

"Of course you didn't," said Tony. He went to her and put an arm about her ample waist.

"That's all very well, m'lord." Slingsby was like a figure of doom. "But, mean it or not, she's done it. I tell you, my blood fairly boils when I contemplate that young Syd. I've not been accustomed," said the butler bitterly, "to serving in houses where the so-called head of the family offers in the middle of luncheon to examine the guests' scalps and see why their hair is falling out."

Polly gasped.

"Did he do that?"

"He did. And he told Sir Gregory Peasmarch that, if he wasn't careful, he'd soon be 'aving to wear a fur rug."

"Fur rug?"

"A toopay, m'lord," explained the butler.

Tony was impressed.

"I must make a note of that," he said. "Useful. Good telling phrase to work off on the customers."

Ma Price for the first time definitely gave way to her grief. She sobbed undisguisedly.

"Ah, cheer up, Mrs. Price," urged Polly.

"Whatever 'ave I bin and gone and done?" moaned the stricken woman.

The butler glowered coldly.

"I'm telling you what you've been and gone and done. You've 'urled 'is lordship 'ere out of his ancestral home, and you've planted in his place a 'ideous changeling who calls His Grace the Duke of Pevensey an onion."

"Not old Pevensey?" cried Tony, delighted.

"Yes, m'lord. To his face. His Grace was speaking—rather authoritative, as his custom is—and young Syd told him to remember he wasn't the only onion in the mince."

"Just what I've been wanting to tell him myself for years."

Slingsby was reproachful.

"It may please your lordship to treat the matter with levity, but I can assure your lordship that there was a 'ighly painful scene. I thought for a moment His Grace was going to have apoplexy."

"Oh dear, oh dear, oh dear!" moaned Ma Price. She looked with concern at Polly. Clearing the table, Polly had left the champagne bottle. She now picked it up and moved to the door. "You be careful of that stuff, Polly," said Ma Price. "Keep off it! The 'arm it does!"

Polly went out with the bottle. Her departure seemed to give Slingsby the comforting feeling of being in a position to thresh out a family difficulty with no strangers present.

"Now, then, you!" he said briskly. "Let's have this straight. What are you going to do about it?"

"Oh dear, oh dear, oh dear!"

"Stop it, you yowling old nuisance!"

Tony intervened.

"Steady, Slingsby. Temper your acerbity with a modicum of reserve."

"M'lord." The butler checked him with a reproving glance. "Well?"

His erring sister sniffed.

"Me 'ead's goin' round so, Theodore, I 'ardly know *what* to do for the best."

"You 'ardly know? Of course you know. And if you don't know, I'll tell you. Ebsolutely decline to give evidence. Wash out your fairy story. Cancel the 'ole thing."

"Well, maybe." Ma Price looked doubtful.

"I'm on me way to the chapel now—to pray for guidance. Polly, my dear," she said, as the girl came in, "I'm off to the chapel to pray for guidance. Come with me as far as the corner, dearie."

"All right, Mrs. Price."

Ma Price wiped her eyes.

"I might have known," she said, "that disaster and trouble was going to 'appen. The very morning I went down to Langley End I broke a mirror."

"You shouldn't have looked in it," said Slingsby.

Tony eyed him, awed, as the door closed. Having known the butler hitherto only in his professional capacity, with the suave mask of office concealing anything in the way of the more tempestuous emotions, he found matter for astonishment in this new Slingsby. He had not supposed that a butler could get off anything half as snappy as that last crack; and he was impressed, as one always is when one's fellow man reveals unsuspected depths.

"You're a hard man, Slingsby," he said. "A great cross-talk artist, but a hard man."

The butler breathed heavily.

"I feel hard, m'lord. When I think of all the harm that old josser has done, I fairly bristle."

Tony started.

"Bristle? Would you like a shave?"

"No, thank you, m'lord."

Tony sighed. Life seemed to be nothing but frustration.

"I'm dying to shave somebody. A barber's not a barber till he's drawn blood."

The butler frowned—respectfully but rebukingly.

"I don't like to hear your lordship talk that way."

"Sorry," said Tony. "We professionals, you know. You can't keep us off shop."

He paused, startled. A loud and unexpected snort had suddenly proceeded from his companion. At the same time, a dark flush had crept over his face. Turning, Tony perceived the reason. During his last remark, a dejected-looking figure had manifested itself in the doorway. It wore riding clothes, but not that air of jauntiness which usually goes with the costume.

"Well, as I live and breathe," cried Tony, "the fifth Earl in person! Come in, old thing."

Syd did not acknowledge the invitation. He

was staring with gloomy hostility at the butler. In the interval of his probation at Langley End, the always rather marked antagonism between these two seemed to have become intensified. It would have been hard to say which of the pair was looking at the other with the greater dislike.

"Oh!" he said. "You're 'ere, are you?"

"Yes, I'm here," replied the butler grimly.

The scowl darkening Syd's face grew deeper. "Plotting and sneaking, as usual, I suppose?"

"Young Syd . . . !"

"Me lord to *you!*"

"Gentlemen," said Tony soothingly, "please!" He turned hospitably to the newcomer. "Take a seat."

"Rather stand."

"Really? Any special reason?"

"Yes," said Syd briefly. "Riding lessons."

Tony was sympathetic. He understood.

"Hurts a bit at first, doesn't it? Never mind. You'll soon be a horseman."

"A corpse, more likely. Why, blimey, I've been thrown so much, I'm not a man, I'm just a solid bruise in 'uman shape."

He paused. He seemed to be wondering whether to take notice of the very unpleasant laugh which had just escaped Slingsby. Deciding, on consideration, not to lower himself by doing so, he proceeded.

"I'm told," he said, addressing his remarks to Tony, "that two of my ancestors was killed in the 'untin' field."

Tony nodded.

"Quite right. One grandfather. One uncle. Two in all."

"Things like that is apt to go in threes," said Syd gloomily.

"Ah, well, *noblesse oblige.*"

"What say?"

"Let it go," said Tony.

The butler forced his way into the conversation.

"Serves you right, young Syd. Apin' your betters."

"I don't want any back-talk from you, you menial."

"Gentlemen!" said Tony.

Syd frowned.

"It's Ma's fault," he said querulously. "If she had told the trufe when I was younger, it would all 'ave come about natural."

"A man's what he is . . ." said Slingsby.

"Will you stop putting in your oar?"

"A man's what he is," repeated the butler firmly, "and anyone that gives up every thought and 'abit to make himself something different will end up nothing but a trained monkey. When you've learned all your lessons and made yourself over, you're going to be like some 'orrible old woman that's had her face lifted—afraid to smile for fear something will crack."

Syd gulped.

"You don't expect me to give up my rightful in'eritance, do you—fathead?"

"Don't you call me fathead."

"Well, *somebody's* got to."

"Gentlemen!" said Tony. "Gentlemen!"

Slingsby, after the last exchange, had come to the conclusion to which he had been forced so often in the past, that there was not much change to be got out of Syd in a verbal contest. The wiser policy was to ignore him. He did so, pointedly.

"I will bid you good-day, m'lord," he said heavily. "I'm going."

"Yes, perhaps you'd better," agreed Tony, "before bloodshed sets in. Look in again some time."

"Thank you, m'lord."

The butler gave Syd a haughty glance and stalked out.

"So they've been putting you through your paces, eh?" said Tony.

"*'Ave* they?" Syd's face twisted. His manner resembled that of some victim of the Inquisition who, released from the torture chamber, has been asked by an interested friend how it all came out in there. "Lumme, there isn't a minute that one of 'em isn't after me—telling me to act contrary to my instinks." He sighed. "I know it's kind of them, of course. They're only tryin' to be 'elpful."

"What's the programme, as a rule?"

Syd pondered.

"Well, take to-day. Visit to the tailor with my brother Freddie. Riding in the Row with Freddie at two-thirty. 'Ighbrow concert with Lady L. at five. Some sort of a lecture somewhere after dinner. And when all the others are through with me, I'm turned over to that Slingsby for lessons in foods and wines. 'Ow they're eaten and drunk—why—when—and what with."

"If you're riding with Freddie at two-thirty, won't you be a bit late?"

"I'll be more than late." Syd gave a bitter laugh. "I won't be there. I've given him the slip."

"And here you are, back on the old spot."

"R!" Syd inhaled deeply. "Smells good, don't it?"

"So you've missed the shop?"

The innocent question seemed to have the effect of sounding an alarm in Syd's soul. He shot a quick glance at Tony, a glance both wary and defensive, as one suspecting a trap.

"Oh, no," he said, with a feeble attempt at nonchalance. "Just thought I'd look in."

"I see."

"We Droitwiches are like that—impulsive. And there's one or two things I'd like to fetch from my old room. Any objec?"

"None at all. Nothing's been moved."

"You living up there now?"

"No, I sleep at my club."

"Ma . . ." He corrected himself. "Mrs. Price still there, I suppose?"

"Yes. She's out at the moment. Gone to her chapel."

"I'd like to see Mrs. Price again," said Syd wistfully.

"Stick around, and you will. By the way," said Tony, "when you come back, would you like me to give you a shave?"

Syd stared.

"Let you shave me? No, thanks. I'm not tired of life."

"Come, come! This isn't the spirit of the Crusading Droitwiches."

"I don't care what it is," said Syd firmly. "Safety First's my motto. You take my tip and don't try shaving till you're fitted for it. If you want to do anything, cut 'air. Then you won't go murdering anybody. And if you do cut 'air, don't get carried away and try singeing. Singeing requires a steady 'and."

With this maxim, he withdrew.

"Singeing requires a steady 'and," murmured Tony. "I'm learning something every day."

He was still meditating on this cardinal truth when he was interrupted by the arrival of another visitor.

"Hullo, Tony, old top," said Freddie in the doorway.

Chapter Fourteen

FREDDIE had changed his clothes since his first visit to the shop and was now dazzling in a natty riding-suit. He gazed at Tony with solemn affection.

Tony was delighted to see the once-familiar face.

"Old Freddie, by Jove! Come on in and have some hair oil. I'd offer you champagne, but the bottle's gone."

"You're looking dashed fit, Tony. I was in here this morning. Did they tell you?"

"Yes. Sorry you went away before I got back. I could have given you lunch."

"I lunched with Tubby Bridgnorth and his future father-in-law. The old man's richer than Rockefeller and balder than an egg."

"What egg?"

"Any egg."

"But why mention the poor fellow's misfortune to me?"

"I've been recommending Price's Derma Vitalis to him, and I think he's interested."

"What a pushful young devil you are," said Tony admiringly. "I see. Of course, that'll do me a bit of good."

"Why you?"

"I own the stuff, don't I?"

Freddie chuckled.

"Don't be an ass, old boy. You won't be in this shop much longer."

"You really think there's a chance of Syd not pressing his claim?"

"A chance?" Freddie emitted another chuckle. "Old boy, it's a cert. The man's weakening visibly. He was talking to me last night about his old life as a care-free barber. He raved with tears in his eyes about Southend and games of darts and skittles and coconut shies and winkles and jellied eels . . . I tell you, the feller is pining, positively pining."

He broke off suddenly. His wanderings about the shop had brought him in front of the mirror, and he stood there gazing at his reflection. One elegant hand came up and brushed itself against the chin.

"Hullo!"

"What's the matter?"

"I need a shave."

Anybody who had ever seen a war horse start at the sound of the bugle would have been irresistibly reminded of that sight by Tony's reaction to this remark. His body twitched. An excited gleam came into his eyes. He licked his lips furtively.

"Do you?" he said in a hushed voice, such as Moses might have used when seeing the Promised Land from the summit of Pisgah. "So you do!"

Freddie had not observed these manifestations. He had lowered himself into the chair and was lying there with his head back.

"Where's that chap I spoke to this morning? Feller with specs."

"You mean Meech, late of Truefitt's?"

"That's the bird. Ring for him and let him get busy. I haven't too much time."

"Leave the whole thing to me," said Tony.

He swathed his victim in a sheet, and began to strop a razor. Freddie sat up, alarmed.

"What are you doing?"

"Just getting things ready. Saves time."

"Oh."

Freddie sank back, relieved; and Tony began to mix the lather. There was rather a solemn look on Tony's face. There had been moments in the past—as, for instance, on the occasion when the other had sneaked his pet brassie and broken it—when he had wondered why Freddie had been sent into the world. Now he knew. And the realization that Providence does nothing without a purpose awed him.

Freddie had begun to chuckle again.

"I say."

"Hullo?"

"We've been making young Price ride."

"Oh?"

"You ought to see him. He comes off like a sack of coals."

Tony, though occupied with the task of lathering his client's face, found time to administer a word of warning.

"You be careful, my lad. Suppose he breaks his neck."

"Don't make my mouth water, old boy. Pf-ff-ff!"

Tony suspended the lathering, and eyed him inquiringly.

"What's the matter? Mouth watering?"

"You're filling me up with soap, you silly ass."

"Sorry. Lathering's like singeing. It requires a steady 'and."

He completed the lathering. Syd, returning from his quest, was in time to see him reach for the razor and stoop over the unconscious victim. Freddie always closed his eyes when he was being shaved, and he did so now. He did it with an easy mind, for he had heard the door open as Syd entered and supposed that here at length was the feller with the specs. No inkling of his doom was upon him. At the moment, indeed, he was musing dreamily on the question of whether a good, straightforward, old-fashioned Dry Martini wasn't better, when you came right down to it, than all these Stick 'Em Up's and Lizard's Tonsils and what not that they were so fond of mixing nowadays.

Into this reverie stole the gentle voice of Tony.

"You know, Freddie," said Tony pensively,

"it must be a big moment in a barber's life—
the first customer he doesn't cut."

Freddie opened his eyes. He started up. He
resembled some wild creature of the woods that
has perceived the trap beneath the leaves.

"Here, I say! Dash it!"

"It's all right, old man."

"All *right?*"

Syd could endure no more. He had been
fidgeting restlessly during the last few moments,
the old warrior yearning to get in to the fray.
The sight of the lather, the smell of the lather,
the whole scenic effect had stirred to life
irresistible cravings within him.

He dashed forward with a cry.

" 'Ere! Gimme that!"

He snatched the razor from Tony's hand and
stood there facing them—stern, defiant, resolute,
like Roland gripping his great sword at Ronce-
valles.

"It fair sets me teeth on edge," he said,
"watching an amatoor."

Freddie, instead of thanking heaven with
raised eyes for his escape, was exclamatory and
indignant.

"Hullo!" he cried. "What the deuce are you doing here?"

"Get back in that chair."

"Yes, but, dash it . . ."

"Sit still, will you," said Syd, between set teeth. Gone was the dejection which had marked his entrance ten minutes back. That air of being a football of Fate—and a well used football, at that—had left him. He was strong, dominant, a man doing his own job on his own ground.

Freddie appeared to resign himself. The question of why Syd was in Mott Street, Knightsbridge, instead of with the horses at Prince's Gate, he seemed to have decided to go into later. He was a young man of common sense. He needed a shave. He was about to be shaved by an expert. Let the thing, he reasoned, go on.

He closed his eyes and leaned back in the chair again.

"Carry on," he said briefly.

Tony was regarding the man behind the razor with exaggerated surprise.

"Why, Lord Droitwich!" he exclaimed.

Syd flashed him a cold look.

"Yes, I *am* Lord Droitwich," he said doggedly, "and don't let anyone tell you different. But I've been aching to shave someone for weeks."

"I know the feeling."

"You watch me now."

"I'm watching."

"You can learn a lot from seeing an artist at work."

Tony drew closer.

"I get the idea," he said. "The overlapping grip and plenty of follow-through."

Syd was breathing tensely. So might a surgeon have breathed, midway through a major operation. He took a pride in his work.

"Watch me," said Syd. "You got to study the grain of the 'air—the way it goes—see?—and follow it, like this." He shaved Freddie masterfully. "Go the other way, and what happens?"

He had addressed the question to Tony, but Tony, had he but known it, did not constitute his entire audience. During these professional remarks, a little group of three had entered the shop, unseen by either Tony or himself. The first to enter was Lady Lydia Bassinger, followed immediately by Violet Waddington and Sir Herbert. The idea of paying a call upon

Tony on their first day in London had occurred to them instinctively, as it had occurred to Freddie. And the spectacle of the young man so soon—unless some fortunate miracle happened—to be Lord Droitwich engaged in shaving in the old shop struck them momentarily dumb.

"Go the other way," continued Syd, "and what 'appens? You drag out the follicles by the roots. I 'ad a lad working for me once . . . a lad by the name of Perkins . . . and could I teach him to follow the grain? Not in a million years. I said to him till I was sick and tired, 'Young Alf,' I said, 'will you or will you not . . .'"

The story, which would probably have had a very valuable moral, was never completed. For at this moment Lady Lydia's pent up feelings got the better of her, and she expressed them in a monosyllabic ejaculation.

"Well! ! !" said Lady Lydia.

Chapter Fifteen

As all fair-minded people know, an artist must be judged by his work as a whole, not by his occasional failures. We cannot, therefore, point the finger of censure at Syd Price because on this one occasion he was guilty of nicking a customer's chin. His record as the best shaver west of the Marble Arch still stands.

Nevertheless, this is what he did. The sudden interruption had had a disintegrating effect on him. His practised razor slipped, and Freddie, bounding from the chair with a howl of anguish, buried his face in a towel and filled the air with bitter reproaches.

Syd scarcely noticed the catastrophe. He was staring pallidly at the intruders.

Tony was the first to speak.

"Well, well, well!" said Tony. "Just one big family!"

Lady Lydia accorded him but a momentary glance.

"How are you, Tony dear?" she observed briefly, and returned her gaze to Syd. "So this is how you behave when we take our eyes off you for a moment!"

Tony took the unfortunate young man by the elbow and led him forward.

"Eliza," he said, "meet the bloodhounds!"

Freddie was full of his own troubles. He was scrutinizing himself in the mirror, goggle-eyed with concern.

"See what you've done?" he cried, his voice trembling with self-pity. "Nasty flesh wound! And you call yourself a barber."

Syd might have replied that even barbers are subject to sudden spasms when addressed unexpectedly from behind in the middle of their work, but he took a different angle.

"I don't call myself a barber. I call myself an earl."

Sir Herbert snorted.

"A pretty earl!"

Tony studied Syd's profile doubtfully.

"Would you say that?" he asked.

"A nice sort of earl!" said Sir Herbert. "Shaving!"

"I *thought* he was yearning for a taste of his native bay rum."

This was Violet. Nobody liked Violet much, and the remark perhaps explains why.

Syd had now recovered his fortitude sufficiently to argue. Confidence began to return to him as he did so. He knew himself to be at his best as an arguer.

"All right, all right, all right!" said Syd. "I'm sorry. I can't help it, can I, if I'm carried away by impulse? All the Droitwiches have been impulsive. I come here to fetch some things from my room and, 'appening to see me young brother about to 'ave his throat cut, I pushed in. No 'arm in that, is there?"

"Not if you don't think Freddie ought to have his throat cut," said Tony.

"It *is* cut," said Freddie vehemently. "I'm spouting like a fountain."

Syd's animation died away. Sorely oppressed these last two weeks, he cracked under the strain. He laid the razor down and made a wide gesture of despair.

"Oh, to 'ell with it all!" said Syd. "I'm fed up."

He slouched to the window and looked out, his back the back of one who has suffered enough.

Sir Herbert and Lady Lydia exchanged a conspiratorial, husband-and-wife look.

"I see," said Lady Lydia. There had been a pause, and she spoke quietly and without her former truculence. Her manner now was that of a good woman stricken to the core by an ingrate. "You're tired of being trained to your position? You do not appreciate all we are doing for you? Well, of course, if you don't *want* our help . . ."

Syd became galvanized into mobility again. He turned quickly, his face alarmed.

"Oh, I'm not sayin' that."

"Then what the devil do you mean, sir," demanded Sir Herbert heatedly, "by acting in this way? You're supposed to be riding in the Row, and we find you sneaking off to this shop to indulge in your vulgar pursuits . . ."

"What's the use," asked Lady Lydia, "of our taking all this trouble to educate you if . . ."

"I'm sorry."

Tony shifted uncomfortably. Until now, he had been amused. He liked his comedy vigorous, and the spectacle of Freddie shooting from that chair had pleased and entertained him. But now, for the first time, he began to be aware that the situation had a pathetic side. He looked at Syd. The poor devil was absolutely cringing. Tony bit his lip.

Lady Lydia did not share his qualms. She was continuing the assault.

"I really feel like giving you up completely."

Syd gazed at her piteously.

"Oh, don't say that. I just got dis'eartened for a bit. Seemed to me," he said unhappily, "I couldn't do anything right, and I began to wonder if the apple was worth the stomach-ache."

"A revolting metaphor," said Lady Lydia, closing her eyes.

"If the jam was worth the powder, I *should* have said."

"A very slight improvement."

Freddie was still wrapped up in his own private tragedy.

"The bleeding's stopped," he announced. "Now what? Lockjaw, I suppose."

"I'm sorry," mumbled Syd.

"Too late to be sorry now," said Freddie gloomily.

Lady Lydia brought the conversation back to its former theme.

"Well, we won't discuss it any longer," she said. "Go and get your ride."

"My ride?" said Syd pallidly. He had had a faint hope that in the general uproar and confusion the matter of his riding had been forgotten.

"Murgatroyd has been waiting at Prince's Gate with the horses since half-past two."

"And if you have no respect for the name of Droitwich," said Sir Herbert explosively, "at least have some for a horse."

Even Freddie, though practically a dismembered corpse, as you might say, was impressed by this.

"Good heavens, yes," he said. "They must be getting frozen stiff. Come on."

What Tony had called the spirit of the Crusading Droitwiches had ceased entirely to animate the unhappy young man who claimed to be their descendant. Syd seemed petrified.

"I can't do it," he pleaded. "And if you was

to see my bruises you wouldn't have the heart to make me. Why, my right thigh looks more like the painting of a sunset than a yuman leg."

"I move," proposed Violet, "that the gentleman shows us his right thigh."

Again Tony moved uneasily. He was feeling as he had sometimes felt when watching a one-sided boxing contest. This thing wasn't fair.

"Bruises or no bruises," said Sir Herbert portentously, "you have got to learn to ride. Are you aware that as the Earl of Droitwich you will naturally become M. F. H. of the Maltbury?"

"I suppose you think," chimed in Lady Lydia, "that a Master of Hounds can attend meets on a bicycle?"

Syd was growing sullen under the barrage.

"If I 'ad my way, I'd stop the Maltbury 'Unt and shoot the foxes."

A heavy silence followed the remark. Sir Herbert turned with a dreadful calm.

"It's no good, Lydia," he said. "We shall have to give him up as a bad job. He must stew in his own juice. If he doesn't want to be fitted for his position, let him do as he pleases."

Defiance left Syd. He capitulated in a panic.

"I'll go," he said desperately. "I'll go. Thank 'eaven the dirt in the Row looks fairly soft."

"Wait a minute," said Tony.

His usually cheerful face was clouded, as he stepped forward. He intended to put this thing right.

"Wait a minute," he said. "Listen, Syd, you poor, misguided ass. They're making a fool of you."

"Tony!" ejaculated Lady Lydia.

"There's no earthly need for you to ride if you don't want to."

Syd had stopped on his way to the door and was regarding him with narrowed eyes. A Cockney to the marrow, he had the Cockney's ingrained suspicion of sudden friendliness.

"What makes you say that?"

"I'm sorry for you."

"Oh?" Syd laughed bitterly. "Think you're clever, don't you?"

"What do you mean?"

"I'm onto you all right," said Syd, with the air of a good man exposing and baffling a human serpent. "You'd like me not to learn, wouldn't you? You'd like them to stop 'elpin' me and let me be a laughing-stock before my case comes up next month. That would suit your book proper, eh? Well, I'm goin' ridin', see? Even if I end up with sunsets all over me."

"Don't forget the concert at five," said Lady Lydia.

"Concert?" Syd's jaw dropped. "Gawd! I'd forgotten. All right, Auntie, I'll be there. . . . What a life!"

He crawled out, a battered martyr. Freddie, with one last look at himself in the mirror, followed. The immediate future was almost as black to him as his unwilling riding mate.

"I'll look nice in the Row, I don't think!" said Freddie gloomily. "With a bally six-inch sabre-cut all across my face!"

Chapter Sixteen

INSIDE the shop, the Family Council's austerity had relaxed in a hum and flurry of delighted self-congratulation. Sir Herbert, who during the recent scene had worn the aspect of a stern judge confronted with a particularly low type of criminal, was once more the genial country gentleman Nature had intended him to be. Lady Lydia and Violet were smiling happily.

Only Tony stood aloof from the rejoicing group. His face was still clouded, and he eyed the merrymakers sourly.

"Capital!" said Sir Herbert.

"Yes, I must say," agreed Violet. "you seem to have got him on the run."

"Another week," said Sir Herbert, "and he'll throw up the sponge."

Lady Lydia was beaming at Tony. Violet also gave him a look of approval.

"That was a master stroke of yours, Tony," she said, "pretending to be sorry for him."

"Yes," said Lady Lydia. "It was very clever of you, dear."

"Positively Machiavellian," said Violet. "I had no notion you were so subtle."

Tony showed no sign of entering into the jovial spirit of the occasion.

"Would it interest you," he asked, "to hear that I meant exactly what I said?"

"What!"

"I *am* sorry for him."

Sir Herbert's geniality waned.

"What are you talking about?"

"Tony," said Violet, "you're dithering."

"I'm sorry for the poor devil, I tell you," repeated Tony stubbornly. "I never liked this scheme of harrying and badgering him, and now I think it's rotten."

Lady Lydia almost bleated in her agitation.

"It's the only way to make him give up his claim."

"I don't care. It's not sporting."

"Sporting!" snorted Sir Herbert.

"Well, it isn't," said Tony. "And I should have thought the only excuse for people like us

is that we're sportsmen. Every time, in the old
days, that I got a twinge of conscience at the
thought that I was living off the fat of the land
and doing nothing to deserve it, I used to con-
sole myself by reflecting, 'Well, at least, I'm
a sportsman!' And here I am, lending myself
to a conspiracy to cheat this poor little blighter
out of his rights."

Sir Herbert was too stunned even to snort
now.

"You're talking like a fool!"

"He's talking," said Violet acidly, "like one
of those men on soap-boxes in the Park."

"I don't care how I'm talking," said Tony.
"I daresay I do sound like a Hyde Park orator.
But you can't get away from the fact that we're
playing a dirty game."

"May I point out . . ." Pomposity had
descended upon Sir Herbert again like a fog.
"May I point out that we are doing it entirely
for your benefit?"

"Yes," said Lady Lydia. "You seem to have
forgotten that."

" 'Blow, blow, thou Winter wind,' " said
Violet. " 'Thou art not so unkind as Man's in-
gratitude.' "

If she intended by lapsing into a rather grisly playfulness to lighten the atmosphere and bring a smile to the face of her betrothed, she failed signally. Tony shot a malevolent look at her. More than ever before, he was wondering how he had ever come to make a fool of himself with this loathsome girl.

"Oh, for God's sake," he snapped, "don't be funny!"

Violet froze.

"I beg your pardon," she said icily.

Tony appealed to Sir Herbert. A certain blindness to the sportsmanlike he could forgive in Woman, but he had always regarded the baronet as a rigid follower of the Code.

"Can't you understand what I mean?" he asked helplessly. "Can't you see that it's brutal to force a man to go riding who even refuses to sit on a cushioned chair?"

"The surgeon's knife, my boy."

"Oh, you make me sick!"

There was a startled silence.

"Well, upon my word . . . !" said Sir Herbert, purple and offended.

Tony had sufficient sense of what was fitting to apologize.

"I'm sorry. I shouldn't have said that. But . . . dash it . . ." He groped for words that would force his point of view through this poison-cloud of prejudice. "Is it cricket?" he asked pleadingly.

Lady Lydia caught at the word with the skill of a practised dialectician.

"Of course it isn't cricket. It's something much more serious."

"Don't you realize," demanded Sir Herbert, "that if this fellow wins his case it will be a menace to the whole peerage?"

"What rot! There have been common men in the peerage before."

"They didn't represent a tradition. Droitwich does. Here we've been for centuries saying that blood will tell and talking about the sacred heritage of birth, and along comes this fellow with the blood of God knows how many earls in his veins acting like a costermonger and calling people onions."

"And the whole British social system," said Lady Lydia, "rests on the principle that a man with his ancestry *can't* be a vulgarian."

Tony refused to yield an inch.

"I don't care. Heaven knows I'm not particularly fond of Syd, but he's entitled to a square deal."

Violet's tight lips twitched. Her eyes gleamed with the cold, militant purpose which had enabled her father to push his Ninety-Seven Soups to triumph in the teeth of a hostile world.

"Then, cutting out the oratory," she said, "what exactly do you propose to do?"

"I propose to tell Syd the truth."

"Which is . . . ?"

"That he can act as he pleases. That an earl doesn't necessarily have to ride if he doesn't want to . . . or go to concerts . . . or be a model of deportment and all the virtues."

"In other words," exploded Sir Herbert, "ruin all our chances!"

"I think you must be insane," said Lady Lydia.

Tony smiled wryly.

"Probably inherited from my great-grandfather," he said. "You've heard about him? Mad Price, they used to call him. He had a shop in St. James's and enjoyed the patronage of the Marlborough Club. But he frittered his fortune away on a visionary scheme for inventing a patent depilatory, and the Bond Street people stepped in and took the trade away from us. That's how we come to be in Knightsbridge."

"A little while ago," said Violet, "you were asking me not to be funny. Might I make the same request of you?"

Tony nodded.

"All right. Comedy over. Now what?"

"Now what?" said Violet. "Well, now perhaps you'll devote a moment to considering *my* position."

"Yes," said Sir Herbert. "Where does she come in?"

"For Violet's sake," said Lady Lydia, "you've no right to throw away your best chance of winning."

Tony was silent for a moment. He looked at Violet.

"I see. Of course, I don't suppose you will want to marry a barber."

"You suppose right."

"So if I tell Syd the truth you'll give me the chuck?"

"Trying to put me in the wrong, eh?"

"Not at all. I . . ."

"Well, I don't care," said Violet. "It's all right. Leave it at that. If you are so superlatively honest that you insist on helping to put this man in a position which you know as well as I do he's entirely unfitted for . . ."

"That isn't the point."

". . . and won't be happy in."

"That isn't the point, either."

Violet's eyes were frozen.

"Well, *my* point," she said, "is that, if you do, I'm through. Is that clear?"

"Quite," said Tony.

Sir Herbert was appalled. As Earl of Droitwich, Tony would be quite comfortably provided with this world's goods, but by no means so well provided—what with Death Duties and Land Taxes and all the rest of it—as to be in a position lightly to sever relations with the heiress of Waddington's Ninety-Seven Soups.

"Now, now, listen," he pleaded. "Surely there is no need to . . ."

He broke off, his music still within him. What powerful argument he was about to put forward, what Grade A oil he intended to throw on the troubled waters, will never be known. Polly Brown, having seen Ma Price as far as the corner, had made her way back to the shop. She was now standing by the door, well within earshot of this intensely private and delicate family debate.

She seemed embarrassed at having plunged into the mob scene.

"Oh . . . I beg your pardon . . ." she began.

"Come right in," said Tony. "We've said all we're going to say. Get her off all right?"

"Yes."

"Who?" asked Sir Herbert.

"My lady mother," explained Tony. "Polly escorted her to the chapel."

Violet looked at Polly.

"Polly?" she said silkily. "How nice to know your Christian name."

"What," asked Lady Lydia, puzzled, "does that woman want in chapel on a Saturday?"

"Oh, we pray all the time, we Prices," said Tony.

A great idea flashed upon Lady Lydia.

"Herbert!" she cried.

Violet was still interested in Polly.

"I suppose," she was saying, "you and Lord Droitwich have been seeing quite a lot of each other lately?"

"Yes," said Polly.

"How nice!" said Violet.

"Herbert!" cried Lady Lydia, inspired, "I have an idea. *Now* is the time to go to that awful old woman and try to make her see reason."

A hint of what was passing in her mind seemed to convey itself to Sir Herbert.

"By gad! You mean . . . ?"

"If we meet her as she comes out of chapel, we may catch her in a weakened state . . ."

"By Jove, you're right!"

Lady Lydia turned to Polly, breathing quickly. In spite of Tony's mad attitude, victory might yet be achieved at the eleventh hour. Lady Lydia knew the Ma Prices of this world. It is notorious that never are they so amenable to the voice of Reason as when they have just come out of chapel. Catch them then, and they are as malleable as putty.

"Where is this chapel?"

"Just down the first street to the left."

"Lydia!" cried Sir Herbert, with as much animation as if he had just discovered a fox stealing out of a spinney. "Come on!"

Nor was his mate backward. It was as if she, also, had discovered it.

"With you, Herbert!" she replied, and the words were a View Halloo.

"This is our big chance," said Sir Herbert emotionally. "We mustn't miss her."

They shot out of the shop like hounds on the scent. Tony turned to Violet.

"Aren't you going with them?"

His manner was distant. So was Violet's.

"I have some shopping to do. I'll leave my car outside and come back for it."

She walked to the door.

"You'll think over what I said?"

"I will."

Violet stared at Polly. It was an unpleasant stare.

"Of course," she went on, "when I said it, I didn't realize all the attractions of life in Price's barber-shop."

"The traditions?"

"The society," said Violet. "Good-bye."

Chapter Seventeen

THE abrupt departure of the heiress of Waddington's Ninety-Seven Soups, following so closely upon the still more sudden vanishing of Sir Herbert and Lady Lydia Bassinger, had had the effect of making Polly Brown feel a little dizzy. She sat down in the shaving-chair, and directed her gaze in a bewildered stare at Tony. He, at least, seemed solid in a shifting world, though she would not have been surprised if he had followed what appeared to be the current fashion by making an emotional dash for the door. Since her return to the shop, people seemed to have been bolting out of that door like rabbits.

"What was she talking about?" asked Polly.

"Nothing," said Tony. "Just drooling."

His face was illuminated by a happy and contented smile. To Tony, all seemed for the best in the best of all possible worlds. He was free at last, and he expressed his appreciation of the fact by heaving a deep sigh of relief.

Polly was not to be satisfied with off-hand statements like this. She had the sense of having just been caught up in a sort of cyclone. What had caused this cyclone it was beyond her to guess; but she knew an atmosphere of strained nerves and taut tempers when she met one.

"She seemed mad at you," she said.

"She was."

"Why?"

"Why not?"

Polly, womanlike, went straight to the core of the matter. She disapproved of these masculine evasions. She was a girl who liked to know exactly what was what.

"Aren't you engaged any longer?" she asked.

"Not any more," said Tony.

His voice betrayed a profound satisfaction. The happy light in his eye grew brighter as he looked at her.

"Those wedding bells will not ring out," said Tony.

He gazed at Polly fondly. In his dealings

with this girl until this moment he had been shackled and handicapped by the thought that —with Violet Waddington still in the position of one holding and presumably intending to exercise an option on his poor person—he had no right to allow himself that free expression of his feelings without which a lover is a spent force from the start. Now, all obstacles between them had been removed; and Polly, though she was not aware of it, was in the presence of a Conquering Male.

"My engagement, thank goodness," said Tony, "is off."

The occasion seemed one for congratulations, rather than sympathy. Polly inclined her head sagely.

"I think you're lucky," she said.

"So do I."

"I've never met a Society girl yet who hadn't a heart like a cold fish," said Polly, speaking as one who knew. "Of course, she's lovely to look at."

"I suppose she is."

"Still, what's the good of that?"

"Exactly."

Polly's feminine curiosity deepened.

"What made you get engaged to her?"

"Oh, these things happen."

"I suppose so."

A brief silence fell upon the Price tonsorial parlour. From the Brompton Road came the rumble of traffic. London was going about its business and its pleasure, unaware that stirring things were on the verge of happening down Mott Street. Polly got up and looked at herself in the mirror. Tony picked up a copy of the *Tatler* and with it made an absent-minded attempt to swat a passing fly. He missed the fly, which proceeded on its way with a sneer.

Tony put down the *Tatler*.

"I say," he said.

Polly turned.

"Yes?"

Tony gave his tie a jerk.

"Talking of engagements . . ."

"Yes?"

"Meech was speaking to me of his this afternoon."

"Mr. Meech?"

"Yes."

Something thudded on the door. Apparently one of the children whose presence lends such

life and gaiety to Mott Street had flung an old
boot at it. Tony paid no attention. Nor did
Polly. Tony was standing in the middle of the
room, twisting his fingers. Polly had taken up
a bottle of Price's Derma Vitalis and was looking with what seemed to be intense interest at
the directions on the label.

"I always thought Mr. Meech was married,"
she said.

Tony shook his head.

"I admit," he said, "that he has the crushed,
drooping look of a married man, but at present
he's only engaged."

"Oh?"

"Yes. Only engaged, at present."

Polly put down the bottle.

"He's been engaged twice," said Tony.
"Showing that there is hope for everyone."

The child who had flung the boot—or perhaps
another child—now began to scream loudly and
unintelligibly to a second—or possibly a third—
child in the street outside. Polly waited till the
uproar had subsided.

"Why are you so interested in Mr. Meech?"
she asked.

"Not in Meech. Only in his methods."

"His what?"

"His methods. His system. His manner of getting engaged."

"Oh?"

"Very educative it was, listening to Meech on his methods."

"What are they?"

Something of the embarrassment which had been afflicting Tony appeared now to have left him. He replied in the more confident fashion of a man who sees his path clear before him. He had the air of an actor who has been given the right cue.

"Well, apparently," he said, "they vary. With his first young lady, he seems to have been a little cautious."

"Cautious?"

"Allusive, if you know what I mean."

"I don't."

"Well, they were sitting in a cemetery, and he asked her how she would like to see his name on her tombstone."

Polly considered this.

"Not so good," was her verdict.

"And yet, on the other hand," argued Tony, "not so bad. It worked."

"She said she *would* like to see his name on her tombstone?"

"Yes. Not immediately, of course, but after long and happy years."

"And the second one?"

"Ah, that was different. You see, the movies had come along by then."

"What had the movies got to do with it?"

"A great deal. They altered the whole method of attack."

Polly wrinkled her forehead.

"He proposed to her in a picture palace?"

"He did better than that. He had observed her reactions at the pictures when the hero embraced the heroine, and they seemed favourable, so one day he just put his fortune to the test, to win or lose it all. He grabbed her in his arms."

"And kissed her?"

"Kissed her with a fierce passion which seemed to turn her very bones to jelly. At least, I gather that he did. He didn't say so in so many words. He merely said he kissed her. But you know how Meech would kiss."

This time Polly was wholly appreciative. Women notoriously admire a dasher. Meech rose in her estimation. She had never suspected it before, but the man apparently had the authentic fire within him. What matter, she felt, if the moustache droops, if only the soul can soar?

"'At-a-boy!" she said.

"'At, as you very justly remark, a boy," agreed Tony. "Then I take it that of the two methods you prefer the second?"

"Of course."

"You're sure?"

"Quite sure."

"Right ho," said Tony. "I thought I'd ask."

And without further preamble he swooped on her in a masterful, Meech-like manner, picked her up with the gay abandon of a stevedore handling a sack of wheat, and kissed her.

He kissed her a good deal. This was what he had been wanting to do for weeks, and, now that the opportunity had presented itself, he did not skimp. He kissed her mouth, her eyes, her hair, her chin, and the tip of her nose.

"Oh, Polly!" said Tony.

She disengaged herself breathlessly.

"Oh, Tony!" said Polly.

The words were simple, but they conveyed
their meaning without ambiguity. And, if there
had been anything obscure about them, her shining eyes would have acted as interpreters.

The shaving-brushes, the bottles of bay rum,
the razor strops and the advertisements on the
walls looked down on this scene with a detachment that suggested disapproval. Nothing of
this kind, they seemed to be saying, had happened in Price's Hygienic Toilet Saloon since
its inception in the days of the Regency.

"Do you love me?" asked Tony.

"Of course I do."

Tony had become calmer. He sat on the edge
of the shaving-basin, and looked at her with
infinite satisfaction.

"Don't speak in that casual tone," he said,
"as if it was the simplest feat in the world. It's
dashed difficult to love me. No girl has ever
done it before. Now, loving *you* . . . well,
that's pie."

"Is it?"

"Of course it is. Anybody could love you. It
took me about two seconds. The moment I saw
you pop out of those bushes and hurl yourself

in front of my car, I said to myself, 'There's the girl I'm going to marry!'"

"You didn't!"

"I did. Just as early as that."

"But what could you see in me?"

"I liked the graceful way you shot through the air."

Polly nestled against him.

"I wish I hadn't fainted that time," she said in a quiet, wistful voice.

"Why?"

"It would have been so wonderful, feeling that you were carrying me in your arms. I missed it all. The next thing I remembered was lying on the sofa."

"Well, see how you like it now," said Tony.

He picked her up and started round the room. He joggled her up and down meditatively.

"You ought to eat more starchy foods," he said.

"Why?"

"It can't be right for a girl only to weigh about ten pounds."

"I weigh a hundred and five."

"Nonsense!"

"I do."

"Then I must be extraordinarily strong. You feel like a feather. Am I really a sort of godlike bloke, or is it just love that gives me the illusion?"

"You're wonderful! But—oh, Tony."

"What?"

She wriggled from his arms. Her small face was serious. The opalescent mist of happiness was beginning to thin from her eyes. For a brief while she had given herself up completely to the magic of the moment, but now that innate common sense of hers had begun to regain its sway. She was a clear-seeing girl.

"Of course," she said, with a little sigh of sorrow for dreams that must die in the chill awakening, "it's no good."

Tony stared at her, aggrieved. He took deep exception to the remark. It seemed to him a fatheaded remark, unworthy of the queen of her sex.

"No good? What's no good?"

"You can't marry me. You'll have to marry some girl in your own class."

"What do you mean—my class?"

"Well, suppose the Court decides you're an earl?"

"Listen!" said Tony, with emphasis. "Attend carefully to me, wench, and don't let me have to speak of this again. If I'm an earl, you'll be a countess."

"I couldn't."

"You'll have to be. It's catching. Female of earl—countess. Didn't they teach you that at school?"

"But don't you see . . ."

"I'm jolly well sure I won't be an earl if you refuse to be a countess. That is the first stipulation I shall make."

Polly looked at him mistily.

"Do you really like me as much as that?"

"Do I really . . ." Tony choked. "Haven't you been *listening?*" he demanded indignantly.

Polly resumed her dreams.

"Oh, Tony!" she said.

"Oh, Polly!" said Tony. He slipped from the shaving-basin and once more enfolded her in an embrace from which even Meech might have picked up a hint or two. "What an extraordinarily lucky thing our godfathers and godmothers happened to christen us the way they did. Tony and Polly . . . You couldn't have two names that went better together. How nicely they run off the tongue. 'Tony and Polly are coming down for the week-end. . . . What, don't you know Tony and Polly? A delightful couple, Tony and Polly.' "

"Tony and Polly," repeated Polly softly.

"You couldn't keep two names like that apart. It's like pepper and salt . . . or Swan and Edgar . . ."

"Or Abercrombie and Fitch . . ."

"Or Fortnum and Mason . . . or . . ."

He broke off, staring. The shop door had opened, and through it was limping the battered form of the last of a noble line. The fifth Earl of Droitwich had come back again like a homing pigeon to the shop he loved.

Chapter Eighteen

THE great desideratum in a seat on horse-back," says the Encyclopædia Britannica in its admirable article on Equestrianism, "is that it should be firm. A rider with an insecure seat is apt to be thrown by any sudden movement the horse may make." Syd had not actually written this article, but, if interviewed on the subject, these are the exact sentiments he would have expressed. It was only too evident, as he entered, that his mistrust of that noble animal, the horse, had been well founded. His hat was dented, his clothes muddied, and he moved painfully, like a man whom movement dis-tresses. His reluctance to go riding in the Row had plainly been no idle whim.

Tony regarded him with concern.

"Hullo!" he said. "Have an accident?"

"No, thanks," said Syd. "I've had one."

Polly was all womanly sympathy. She had always been fond of her late employer, and the sight of him now awoke all the ministering angel in her.

"Oh, Mr. Price!" she cried. "Say, let me get you some arnica."

Syd checked her with a gesture. He was too preoccupied to notice that she had addressed him by a name which he had definitely abandoned.

"No!" His face twisted. "I couldn't permit any member of the fair sex to put arnica on the spot that's hurting *me*."

In Tony's demeanour there was nothing but compassion. It was many years since he, too, had passed through the kind of experience which had rendered the other so dishevelled; but no man wholly forgets the emotions of learning to ride.

"Poor old Syd, were you thrown again?"

A grimace of great bitterness contorted Syd's face.

"Yes, I was," he said. "But I'm gettin' used to that. What did me in was the horse kicking me."

"Were you kicked?" squeaked Polly.

"Three times in the same place," said Syd moodily. "Most sure-footed animal I ever saw. Blimey, if I sat down now I'd leave an 'oof-print."

Polly, with another little gasp of womanly commiseration, said that she thought Syd had better give up horses. In this she showed her usual good sense. Syd was not of the stuff of which jockeys are made.

"I've given 'em up—don't worry." Another spasm of pain flitted across the sufferer's face. In a moment of absent-mindedness he had backed against the shaving-chair and was evidently standing face to face with his soul. "I never want to see a horse again, except cut up in little bits and stuck on a skewer."

There was a pause. Syd himself seemed to have nothing more to say, and his two companions delicately forbore to intrude on his sorrow with words. Syd removed his hat, and for some moments regarded himself silently in the mirror. He took up a brush and restored his hair to its usual smoothness. Then, with an over-wrought sigh, he turned to Tony.

"Listen," he said. "I want to see you."

"Feast the eyes," said Tony encouragingly.

"Want to have a business talk."

"Go ahead."

Once more Syd regarded himself in the mirror. The sight seemed to fortify him in the resolution which he had taken, for he came to the point without further preamble.

"What was that offer you made me to drop my claim?" he asked. "That day at Langley End, when all this thing first started. A thousand quid a year, wasn't it?"

"I believe it was."

Syd brooded awhile.

"Well, I'm not sayin' I'll take *that*," he resumed, a measure of his native prudence returning to him.

"You said that at the time."

"But it'll do as a figure to start with."

Tony seemed a little puzzled.

"I don't quite understand. How do you mean, a figure to start with?"

"Basis of negotiations, see?"

Tony was now bewildered. The words he had heard appeared capable of but one interpretation, yet he hesitated to put this interpretation on them. In spite of what Sir Herbert and the

others had been saying at the recent conference
which had broken up so abruptly, he could not
bring himself to believe that a few mishaps in
Rotten Row had been sufficient to cause the
other to wish to abandon a contest which was
already won.

"What exactly are you driving at?" he asked.

Syd seemed impatient of this slowness in the
uptake.

"I want to quit," he said briefly.

"Give up your claim?"

"That's it . . . if it's made worth me while."

Tony whistled softly.

"This is very sudden, isn't it?"

"Been comin' on for weeks," said Syd, with
the air of an invalid revealing symptoms.
"Ridin' lessons . . . concerts . . . lectures . . ." He mused bleakly, and in a soft
voice invoked the name of the Deity. "I've had
enough of it. So, if your proposition is right and
we don't have to quarrel about the figure, I'm
through, and you can have the damn title—
and welcome."

It seemed to Polly that she was out of place
at such a momentous parley. High matters of

state were being discussed, and she felt that she had no right to listen to them.

"Shall I go?" she asked.

"Of course not," said Tony.

"Don't pop off on my account," urged Syd.

"But you want to talk . . ."

"We're going to talk," said Tony. "At least, I am. I'm going to talk to this poor, deluded chump like a Dutch uncle. Syd, you old idiot," proceeded Tony forcefully, "listen. Before we take up the question you have raised, I should like you to answer one of mine."

"Go ahead," said Syd, in the sombre manner which now seemed to have settled permanently upon him.

"Well, then, tell me. What exactly is your mental picture of an earl?"

This appeared to give Syd pause for thought. Apparently he was not good at definition.

"Oo . . ." He frowned at an advertisement of Wilbraham's Soothine which hung upon the wall, as if trying to draw inspiration from it. "Well, I don't know . . . 'igh-class sort of feller . . ."

"A cultivated sort of bird?"

"You might put it like that."

"With a taste for concerts and lectures, and at the same time a crack shot, a splendid horseman, a good dancer, a brilliant conversationalist, and an amusing after-dinner speaker."

Again Syd consulted the Soothine advertisement, as if taking advice of counsel.

"Yes," he said. "That's about what the folks told me."

"And you believed them!"

"Well, what's wrong?" demanded Syd.

Tony laughed.

"If you can find one earl who fills the bill, I'll eat my hat. It's a felt Homburg with a brown ribbon."

Syd was staring. The scales had not actually fallen from his eyes, but they were falling.

"What do you mean?"

"Nine earls out of ten," said Tony confidently, as one who knew the breed, "wouldn't be able to tell Brahms from Irving Berlin and wouldn't want to. Seventy per cent. of them never attended a lecture in their lives. Eighty-five couldn't make a speech if you paid them. And, to cap it all, there are at least one or two who can't ride."

Gulping sounds, as of a stranded fish that has

heard surprising news, were proceeding from Syd.

"Then why," he demanded, putting his finger on the bewildering core of the matter, "did they tell me I'd got to make myself over?"

"So that you would be so uncomfortable that you'd do exactly what you started to do just now—take a settlement and quit."

There followed a heavy pause as this revolting truth gradually penetrated to the Claimant's consciousness. When he spoke, it was in the voice of a man whose mind reels at the depths to which human nature can sink.

"Cool" he said.

Tony pressed his point.

"I'm surprised at you letting them fool you like that," he said. "I should have thought you could have guessed from the start what their game was. Look at me—do you suppose I ever went to lectures and concerts? I rode—yes. But then I liked riding. You really are a mug, Syd, aren't you?"

The Claimant shot at him a quick, suspicious stare. He looked as he had looked when Tony had attempted to convince him at their previous meeting. On that occasion, it had seemed to him that there was funny business afoot, and so it seemed to him now. Life had not so trained Syd Price that he could readily appreciate altruism in those who professed the desire to do him a bit of good. Always, he suspected the catch, and sedulously looked for it.

"And why are you telling me all this?" he asked.

"The motto of the Prices is 'Play the game!'"

Syd quivered with righteous indignation.

"Is it?" he cried. "Well, it don't seem to be the motto of the Bassingers. Making a fool of me! . . . Pretending that all they wanted was to help a feller . . ."

Words failed him, and he sought refuge in his customary "Coo!" He was convinced now. There was that about Tony that impelled belief, and he no longer suspected his good faith. If earls were really as Tony had said—and he ought to know—then the black-heartedness of Sir Herbert and Lady Lydia was plain.

Tony attempted to champion the absent ones.

"Oh, you mustn't hold it against them," he said.

"Ho?" said Syd.

"They're fond of me, you see."

Syd would have none of this specious reasoning.

"Me own relations doing the dirty on me!" he muttered, appalled. He had always known that people in Society were a bit thick, but he had never suspected such thickness as this.

"But they don't feel they *are* your relations. Sir Herbert and Lady Lydia and Freddie think I am the real Lord Droitwich."

Syd snorted loudly and bitterly.

"Oh, they do, do they?"

"You can't blame them, really."

A second snort from Syd seemed to indicate that he found it perfectly possible to blame them. He strode forcefully up and down the room. His eyes were gleaming, and his ears had turned a vivid pink.

"Perhaps they think I won't make a good earl?"

"I'm afraid they have got that idea."

Syd snorted for the third time, and this snort eclipsed in violence and volume the previous snorts, establishing a new record for other snorters to shoot at. He was also injudicious enough to raise his hand and bring it down with impressive force on his thigh—a blunder which he was the first to recognize. A sharp howl proceeded from him, and for a moment he stood rubbing the spot in manifest agony.

Then he straightened himself and glared belligerently.

"Oh?" he said. "Well, I'll show them. I'll show the whole pack of them."

"I take it, then," said Tony, "that the offer you started to make to me is cold?"

"As cold as a stepmother's kiss," replied Syd vehemently, rising to unusual heights of imagery. He brooded. "Imagine me lettin' them lead me up the garden like that! Me that always thought I'd an 'ead on me!"

He sniffed vengefully, and for an instant it seemed as if the acoustics of the shop had produced an echo. Then it became apparent that this was not one sniff, but two sniffs.

The second had proceeded from Ma Price, who had just come into the room.

Chapter Nineteen

Her visit to the chapel had plainly done little or nothing to restore tranquillity to Ma Price. Her demeanour, as she entered the shop, was still that of a woman with much on her mind, and heavy stuff, at that. The sniff had been an over-wrought sniff. She moved like one weighed down by a burden.

Syd regarded her with a distrait eye. Many a time during the past two weeks he had felt a nostalgic yearning for the sight of this woman, but now that they had come together again he found himself unable to bestow upon her more than a perfunctory attention. The thought of his wrongs was occupying him to the exclusion of everything else.

" 'Ullo, Ma," he said absently.

Mrs. Price, too, seemed to be prevented by the

pressure of other emotions from doing justice to
this meeting. She, like Syd, had looked forward
to it with wistful eagerness; but she exhibited
none of the animation that might have been expected. If Syd had been in the frame of mind
to observe her closely, he might have detected
in her manner a curious embarrassment. She had
sunk into a chair and was avoiding his eye.

" 'Ullo, Syd," she said.

"You all right, Ma?"

"I've got a neadache."

"I've got an ache meself," said Syd. "Only it's
at the other end."

"Sir Herbert and Lady Lydia went to look
for you, Mrs. Price," said Polly.

Ma Price nodded.

"I seen 'em. I just bin talking to them."

Syd exploded shrilly.

"Oh, you 'ave, 'ave you? Well, I'm looking
forward to a chance of talking to them myself."
His voice rose, and Ma Price, wincing, pressed
a protesting hand to her forehead. "I've something to say to those two, something that'll make
their 'air curl. I'll give them a piece of my
mind. I'll show Sir Rerbert Blooming Bassinger
where he gets off."

"Don't shout, dearie," pleaded Ma Price plaintively, "I've got such a neadache. Polly, my dear, I'm dyin' for a cup of tea."

"I'll go upstairs and make you some."

"In short," said Tony, "Polly will put the kettle on." He went with her to the Ladies' Department door. "I'll come and help. We'll toast muffins together . . . Tony and Polly!"

She slid her hand into his, and they went out. Syd could hear Tony's voice raised in song as he passed through the Ladies' Department and climbed the stairs beyond, which led to the family's living quarters. He did not like it. At such a moment anything in the nature of singing and rejoicing seemed to him out of place and lacking in taste.

And then his mind came back to a matter of greater urgency. He felt a sense of outrage.

"What," he inquired, "did bloomin' Lydia and blasted 'Erbert want to see you about?"

Thus shockingly did he allude to an honoured baronet and the daughter of a hundred earls. But he was deeply moved. If this sinister pair had been seeking Ma Price out, it could have been only with one object.

Ma Price verified his suspicions.

"They were arguin' with me, dearie. Telling me not to give me evidence."

"That was all, was it?" Syd's voice shook. "Merely tamperin' with me star witness on the eve of the trial? Coo! They're a nice lot. As 'igh-principled a brace of snakes in the grass as you'd want to meet in a month of Sundays! I'm not sure I couldn't 'ave them sent to the jug for that."

"Sir 'Erbert seems to feel the 'ole thing very deep, dear."

" 'E'll feel it deeper by the time I've got through with 'im."

" 'E don't seem to think you're quite suited for your exalted position."

"Ho! And why not?" Syd pierced her with a cross-examining counsel's gimlet eye. "Look 'ere," he demanded. "What's your mental picture of an earl?"

Ma Price was bewildered.

"I dunno," she said helplessly.

"You imagine 'e's an 'ell of a josser, don't you—going to concerts with one hand and ridin' mustangs with the other. Well, you're wrong, see? Seventy per cent. of 'em never attended a concert in their lives. And eighty-five . . . I mean, one or two . . . can't ride."

"Well, you know, I suppose," said Ma Price doubtfully.

"Certainly I know. I've been studyin' the question. And all this joss they've been puttin' over on me is so much applesauce. That's straight. I've 'ad it from an expert."

Ma Price was groping on the shelf below the shaving mirror.

"Oh, dear!" she moaned. "Me 'ead's fairly splittin'. Where's that spray of eau-de-cologne you used to keep 'ere?"

"I tell you, I'll make as good an earl as any of 'em."

Ma Price suspended her quest to gaze at him mournfully.

"But will you be 'appy, dearie?"

"Of course I'll be 'appy."

Ma Price sighed.

"You used to be 'appy once. In this very shop. 'Ow long ago it seems now, and it's only two weeks. . . . I can't find that spray."

"Look in the top shelf."

"Remember the teas we used to 'ave? What a

boy you were for the sausage and mashed!" She sighed again. "If you're goin' to be an earl, I won't be able to cook you no more sausage and mashed."

This plainly shook Syd. For an instant, he definitely weakened. Then he was firm again.

"Life," he said Napoleonically, "ain't all sausage and mashed. There's me destiny to be considered."

"Oh, dear, oh dear, oh dear!"

"It's no use cryin' over spilt milk. What is to be will be."

"You used to be so 'appy once, workin' in this shop."

She snivelled wretchedly, and Syd, who had seen the street door open, uttered a warning "Oy!" Violet Waddington had returned from her shopping, and had come, cold and haughty, to interview Tony on the subject of his recent decision. Outwardly cool and unmoved, she was boiling inwardly with an indignation almost as righteous as Syd's.

"Oh!" she said, looking from one to the other. "I wanted to see . . . well, Mr. Price, I suppose I ought to say."

Syd thought her choice of names very proper.

Mr. Price Tony was, and Mr. Price he was jolly well always going to be. He jerked his thumb over his shoulder.

"Price upstairs," he said crisply. "Getting tea with Polly Brown."

Violet's lips tightened.

"How very domestic!" She uttered a sound which was half an exclamation and half a titter. "Well, it would be cruel to interrupt him at such a moment, wouldn't it? Perhaps you will tell him I came back, and suggest that he writes to me. He will understand."

"Oh, 'ere it is, at last," said Ma Price suddenly. She had found the missing spray.

"It's just about a little matter we were discussing when I left," explained Violet. "I want to know what he has decided."

"I'll go and tell him you're 'ere."

"Oh, don't trouble."

"No trouble. And I could do with a cup of tea myself."

"Thank you so much."

"Pleasure mine," said Syd courteously. "Toodle-oo . . . I mean, see you later."

He withdrew. And Ma Price, who was busy

with the spray, felt that something in the nature of an apology was in order.

"You'll excuse me doing this, miss, won't you?" she said, ceasing for a moment to press the trigger. "I've got a neadache."

"I should think everybody has this afternoon," said Violet. "I hope I didn't interrupt a private conversation?"

"Oh, no, miss. We was just talkin'. Syd's set on bein' an earl, and I was tryin' to make him see it wouldn't do."

Violet stared. These, she felt, were deep waters.

"But that's very odd, isn't it?"

"Odd, miss?"

"Well, considering you're the principal witness to prove that he is an earl . . ."

A hunted look had come into Ma Price's face. She quivered miserably.

"Oh, miss!" she moaned. "I wonder whether I done right."

"If you ask me," said Violet, "no! He'll be miserable."

"That's exactly what I thought, miss. So when Sir Rerbert came to me outside the chapel, I done what I done."

Violet could make nothing of this.

"I don't think I quite understand. What did you do?"

Ma Price looked apprehensively at the door. She sank her voice to a whisper.

"Oh, miss," she quavered, "I 'adn't the 'eart to tell Syd just now, but I signed a paper Sir Rerbert wrote out for me, ebsolutely denyin' that there was any truth in my story!"

Chapter Twenty

Sudden elation stuns as effectively as sudden disaster. For an appreciable number of seconds after hearing these words, Violet Waddington stood silent, incapable of speech. Then she gulped and found utterance.

"What!!"

"Yes, miss." Ma Price looked hopefully at her. What she was needing at the moment was a little moral support. "I hope I did right?"

Violet seemed once more to swallow some obstruction in her throat.

"I think you did quite right," she said slowly.

She clicked her teeth on the words which she had intended to add. Tony had come in.

"Your tea's ready, Nannie." He saw Violet, and nodded curtly. "Hullo, Vi."

"Go and get your tea, Mrs. Price," said Violet. "I'm sure you need it."

Ma Price was of the same opinion.

"You never spoke a truer word, dearie," she said. "I could drink a jugful."

Tony followed her to the door and closed it after her. He came back to Violet, feeling a little puzzled. Violet's eye, encountered upon his entry, had surprised him. It was not the eye of the furious and thwarted woman he supposed her to be. It had a light, a warmth.

An explanation of this phenomenon occurred to him. She had returned, he presumed, with the intention of arguing with him and endeavouring to change his purpose with blandishments and soft words. He did not think she was of the temperament to be very good at it, but he stiffened defensively.

He wasted no time. He came to the point at once.

"Well, Vi . . . I've told him," he said, and braced himself for what might follow.

"The whole truth?"

She was looking at him with an odd smile.

"The whole truth," said Tony.

"That was fine of you," said Violet.

Her smile had become a tender benediction. So might a lady of old have smiled on her knight who had proved himself parfait and gentil. She drew closer to him, and pressed her two hands against his arms.

"Did you really think I meant it when I said I'd throw you over if you told him? I only did it to test you, dear. I wanted to see if you were man enough to do the right thing, no matter what the consequences might be."

He stared at her dumbly. There had come upon him the strange sensation he had sometimes had in dreams—that feeling of playing a part in a scene and knowing all the while that it was not really happening. His ears took in the words, but his reason revolted at them. It was incredible that it could be Violet who was talking like this. . . .

"I only did it to test you, dear." . . . It wasn't the sort of phrase she would use. It wasn't the sort of phrase anybody would use. It sounded like a subtitle from an old silent picture.

Moreover, if Violet was really talking like this, where till now had she concealed this wealth of highmindedness and nobility?

She kissed him quickly.

"I must go," she said. "I've a million things to do. Come and see me to-night when you shut up shop."

She turned and walked briskly out, and Tony continued to gape after her. He had hardly noticed the kiss. His mind had been too busy grappling with the major mystery of her words.

And then suddenly his jaw dropped. There had swept over him the realization of what those words meant.

Behind him a voice spoke.

"Tony."

He whipped round. Polly was standing in the doorway. There was a cup in her hand.

"I brought your tea, Tony," she said, in a small voice. "It was getting cold."

Tony was silent. A little gray tinge had come into his face. Then he stretched out his hand automatically.

"Thanks," he said.

He stood looking at her. The silence stretched out interminably. Outside the public house down the street a wheezy piano-organ had begun to play. Omnibuses rumbled in the Brompton

Road. London was still going about its business.

Tony put the cup down.

"I'm not a cad, Polly," he said slowly.

"I know you're not, Tony."

He dropped into a chair. He was feeling giddy.

"You saw that?" he asked.

"Yes."

"You heard what she said?"

"Yes."

Tony's immobility gave way to a sudden wild frenzy. He beat on the arm of the chair with his fist.

"What the devil am I to do?"

Polly said nothing. Her face was pale, and one small tooth was biting into her lip.

"She said if I gave the game away to Syd . . . told him what the family were up to . . . making a fool of him to try to freeze him out . . . she was through with me. I thought that was good enough. I took it for granted she meant it. And now she says she didn't. It was just some damned test . . . I can't back out now."

"No."

"How can I back out?"

"You can't."

"But, Polly! . . ."

"It's bad luck."

"Bad luck!" He laughed hysterically, then suddenly stopped. "I'm sorry," he said. "I'm behaving like a child. But you shouldn't say things like that. They're too funny. A fellow can't help laughing. Losing you—bad luck!" His face twisted. A dull flush came into it. "I won't do it!" he cried. "I'll be damned if I do it. I don't care if I'm a swine and everybody thinks I'm a swine. I'll go to her and explain. I'll tell her what you mean to me. I'll tell her she's got to let me go. I'll . . ."

Polly shook her head.

"You can't."

"But, Polly . . ."

"No. It wouldn't be you."

He slumped back in the chair. The piano-organ was playing a lively march, and his foot tapped unconsciously in time to it.

"You'd never be happy," said Polly, "if you did anything rotten. Nor would I be happy. I never thought she was the sort of girl who would want to marry you if you had nothing in the world. Something for something, I thought was her motto. But I was wrong. She's fine. You can't let her down, Tony."

"But, my God! How are we going to go on all the rest of our lives? You want me. I want you. Years and years . . ."

"You can't let her down. I know that."

"But, Polly . . ."

"I forgot me spray," said Ma Price behind them.

Ma Price tottered into the shop and made for the shelf. Like Polly a few minutes back, she was carrying a cup of tea—a fact which brought an outraged Syd charging in in her wake.

" 'Ere, what's the idea?" demanded Syd.

Ma Price turned.

"I want me spray, dearie."

"You silly old geezer, you've walked off with my cup of tea."

This was news to Ma Price. She looked at the cup, puzzled.

" 'Ave I?"

Syd was agitated.

"I 'ope to Gawd," he said devoutly, "you aren't goin' to go off your onion and suffer loss of memory with the trial coming up in a month's time! That would fairly put the kybosh on it."

It seemed to Ma Price that the moment had come for revelation. She would have preferred to postpone it, but it went to her heart to see the boy in what you might call a fool's Paradise.

She made an odd, bleating sound.

"Syd . . . There's something I'll 'ave to tell you."

"And there's somethin' you'll 'ave to tell the Committee of the 'Ouse of Lords—remember that."

Through the shop door, breaking in on this tense moment, came a group of three. Lady Lydia, followed by Sir Herbert Bassinger and Violet. Syd glared formidably.

"Ho!" he cried. "The Artful Dodgers—male and female! Reading from right to left, Sir 'Erbert and Lady Serpent-Bassinger!"

Baronets are always short with this sort of thing. If Sir Herbert had been of the other sex, one would have said that he bridled. He puffed his chest out and turned a light purple.

"Now, then!" he said. "Now, then!"

"And the same to you, with knobs on!" replied Syd cordially.

"None of that, please!"

Syd laughed hideously.

"None of that, eh? When I know all **about** your nice little plot? Don't make me laugh, I've got a split lip. You think you're going to **freeze** me out of me lawful in'eritance, do you? A fat chance! I'll see it through in spite of you all."

"You won't," said Lady Lydia.

Syd turned to meet this new attack.

"Ho! And why not?"

"Because," said Sir Herbert, "I have here a paper, signed by Mrs. Price and duly witnessed, in which she absolutely denies that there was any truth in her story."

A high-explosive shell falling in the shop might have disconcerted Syd more, but not much more. His jaw fell slowly. He stared at Sir Herbert. He stared at Lady Lydia. Then, turning, he stared at Ma Price, and his eyes were the eyes of Cæsar gazing at Brutus.

"What!!"

Ma Price sniffed uneasily.

"That was what I wanted to tell you, dearie!" she said.

Tony had come forward. He had been a listless spectator of the battle which had ended in the so signal rout of the Droitwich Claimant. One way or another, the thing mattered noth-

ing to him now. Incuriously, he held his hand
out, and Sir Herbert placed the paper in it with
the air of one depositing valuables in a vault.

"Yes," said Sir Herbert. "You take it, Tony.
And for goodness' sake keep it safe."

He moved a step to one side, as if, fearing a
sudden desperate charge, he was determined to
interpose a substantial barrier between Syd
Price and his nephew. Tony walked to the
shaving-chair, and sat on its arm, reading with
a frown.

Ma Price was speaking again.

"I'm sure I 'ope I done right."

"Quite right," said Sir Herbert cordially.
"Quite right. Perfectly right."

"Thank you, Sir Rerbert. That was what the
lady 'ere said."

Tony looked up with a start.

"What lady?"

"This lady, dearie," said Ma Price, indicating
Violet, into whose eyes an expression of sudden
discomfort had crept. "I told her just before
you came in, and she seemed 'ighly pleased at
what I'd done."

"Of course," said Sir Herbert.

"Naturally," said Lady Lydia.

Tony clenched his hands. The paper crackled in his grip.

"You told her just before I came in?" he said. "I see."

For a long instant he stared at Violet. Then, with a short laugh, he turned away.

He understood now. The nobility and high-mindedness at which he had marvelled were explained.

Sir Herbert was rubbing it in.

"Perhaps even you," he said, addressing the crushed man before him, "are capable of understanding that your whole case now automatically falls to the ground?"

A heavy sigh escaped from Syd. He regarded Ma Price loweringly.

"I might have known what would happen if you went to chapel," he said.

Sir Herbert was now striking a more kindly note. He had begun to point out the silver lining.

"Although you recognize now that you have absolutely no claim upon him, I am sure that Lord Droitwich will not prove ungenerous. If, for instance, you wish to move to Bond Street, I have no doubt that he . . ."

He broke off abruptly. The piercing scream which had proceeded from his wife would have silenced a far more able orator.

Then, seeing, he, too, uttered a shattering cry. "Tony!"

Tony was sitting on the edge of the shaving-basin. In his left hand was the all-important document, in his right a lighted taper. And, as they looked, the paper crackled and crumbled in the flame.

"Tony!"

It was Violet who spoke this time, and he looked at her steadily, a half smile on his face. The paper fluttered in ashes to the ground. He got up and brushed his fingers.

"Singeing requires a steady 'and," said Tony.

Chapter Twenty-one

THE morning sunshine, streaming in through the French windows, lit up the drawing room of Langley End with a cheerful flame. It danced among glass and silver. It sparkled on old chairs. It bathed the portrait of Long-Sword in a golden flood. On the last of Long-Sword's line, however, its rays were unable to fall; for Syd, who was not particularly fond of sunshine, had settled himself in a deep chair in the shadows on the other side of the room and was busy reading the Racing Intelligence in his daily paper.

But if there was no sunshine on Syd's exterior, there was plenty in his heart. Fourteen days had passed since the stirring scene in Price's Hygienic Toilet Saloon in Mott Street, Knightsbridge, and on none of those days had he failed to congratulate himself on the sensational outcome of that family gathering. The thing now looked to Syd like a walkover, and he hummed, as he read, in quiet contentment.

The sound of a footstep outside the windows broke in on his pleasant musings: and, lowering his paper and looking over its edge, he perceived Tony. He regarded him with surprise, for he had supposed him to be seventy miles away in London. But it was indulgent surprise. He had nothing against Tony. Sir Herbert and Lady Lydia he had ticked off properly, telling them exactly what he thought of them; and he had also, in a moving scene, dealt faithfully with the Hon. Freddie Chalk-Marshall; but towards Tony he nourished no hostility. He liked him, and considered that he had done the square thing. So, when he spoke, it was with none of the asperity of a householder who sees an uninvited intruder climbing in through his French windows.

"Oh, it's you, is it, young Price?" he said.

Tony touched his forehead respectfully.

" 'Morning, m'lord."

"And what brings *you* 'ere?"

"Sir Herbert summoned me to a conference,"

Tony explained. "I drove down with Polly in the two-seater."

"Polly all right?"

"As right as any girl can expect to be who's marrying me in a week or so."

Syd opened his eyes.

"You two getting married?"

"We are."

"Well, you might do worse."

"But not better."

"She's a nice girl—Polly," Syd went on meditatively. " 'Andy at manicurin', too. She'll be a help to you in the shop."

"You draw a pretty picture of the Barber's Married Life," said Tony. "The devoted helpmeet trimming one extremity of the customer while he trims the other. I like it. It's romantic. Unfortunately, there will be no opportunity for it in my case. Immediately after the ceremony we are going off somewhere to make our fortune. Kenya is a spot we are considering. Planting coffee, you know."

Syd gaped again.

"Eh? But 'ow about the shop?"

"I'm selling the shop."

"What!" Syd's voice expressed incredulous

horror. He was plainly shocked to the core. "You don't mean that?"

"Yes. I have an offer from a man named Pupin."

"My Gawd!" Syd's consternation deepened. "You're not selling Price's to a dago barber?"

"Pupin is a Swiss."

Syd's sallow face had turned a dusky pink. His eyes glowed angrily.

"I don't care if he's a Fiji Islander," he cried, his voice shaking. "The idea of selling Price's to a foreigner—or to anybody, for that matter. Where's your family pride? Why, Price's has been Price's for six generations." He glared at Tony, as might have glared a High Priest at some wretch guilty of sacrilege. His voice grew shrill. "Are you aware that Rowland Hill— him that started penny postage—used to go to Price's? Thackeray still owes us twopence for trimming his whiskers. Why, we once shaved Dr. Crippen!"

Tony shrugged his shoulders.

"Still," he pointed out, "this is a mercenary age, and I need the money."

Syd, who had risen, slumped down in his chair again.

"Oh, well," he said moodily, "it's your affair, after all, not mine."

"Exactly. Well, you'll excuse me, won't you? I must go and look after Polly. She's probably being bitten by a squirrel. You might tell them I've arrived and shall be out in the garden when they want me."

"Who's they?"

"Sir Herbert and gang."

"Oh, the conference?" A short laugh escaped Syd. "What good do you suppose a conference is going to do you?"

"None, I should imagine."

"And you're right."

"Still, you can't blame Sir Herbert for being a die-hard, can you?"

"Don't talk to me about that reptile," said Syd, with feeling. "Tryin' to break me neck, 'orseback ridin'!"

"Just his quiet fun," said Tony. "Well, see you soon, no doubt."

He disappeared into the sunlit garden, and Syd returned to his paper.

But the Racing Intelligence had lost its magic and its power to grip. Syd lay back in his chair and closed his eyes. Above the eyes there was a frown. Try as he might to reason with himself, try as he might to tell himself that the passing of Price's had nothing to do with an Earl of Droitwich, he could not shake off a feeling of bleak depression as he thought of the old shop falling into alien hands. His earliest recollections all centred around Price's. The place was a shrine to him. He could remember playing on the floor—couldn't have been more than three. . . . And that prodigious row there had been when, at the age of six, he had broken a bottle of the Derma Vitalis. . . .

His first shave! . . . What they called a red-letter day that had been. . . .

And now a blooming Swiss would reign where a dynasty of Prices had held the high justice, the middle, and the low. Syd, though a diligent reader of certain magazines and of a certain type of novel, had never happened upon Fitz-Gerald's Omar Khayyám; had he been acquainted with it, he must have been struck poignantly by the passage where the Persian muses upon the tragedy of the lion and the lizard keeping the courts where Jamshyd gloried and drank deep. The parallel was close, indeed.

Price's! . . . Well, of course, Price's was nothing to him now. All the same . . .

A sigh proceeded from him, and he opened his eyes—to perceive the massive form of Slingsby brooding above him. He sat up, annoyed. He had not heard the butler enter the room, and he had the normal man's dislike for being gazed at without his knowledge.

"Well," he demanded, flushing a little, "what do *you* want, Pussyfoot?"

The butler's demeanour was aloof and frosty.

"I came to see if this room was unoccupied."

"Oh?" Syd glanced at his paper again. This, he felt, was the way to treat the man. Nonchalance. Aristocratic disdain. He read for a moment or two before speaking. Then there occurred to him a question which he wished to have answered. "Who," he asked, "is the old bloke with a face like a halibut who drove up just now?"

Slingsby's eye grew, if possible, colder and more like that of a justly incensed frog.

"I fail to recognize the description," he said stiffly, "but Mr. Wetherby, our family solicitor, arrived not long since."

"For the conference, eh? I suppose he's in the

library, lushin' up *my* sherry." Syd laughed unpleasantly, then dismissed the subject with well bred calm. "Doing anything at Ally Pally this afternoon?" he asked.

Slingsby had, as a matter of fact, spent more than an hour since breakfast meditating over the relative chances of the various horses running that day at Alexandra Palace and, had his interlocutor been someone else, would have welcomed eagerly the opportunity of discussing form. To racing chatter with Syd he declined to stoop. He remained coldly silent.

Syd was scrutinizing the paper.

"Better 'ave a bit on Swiss Cheese for the three-thirty," he advised. "It's a snip."

The butler swelled.

"I want no snips from you."

"Given up betting, 'ave you?" said Syd. "Good thing, too. A man in my position don't want to feel he's got a gambling butler in his employment. Makes him uneasy about the spoons."

Slingsby gulped. Just as his past life flashes through the mind of a drowning man, so now through the butler's mind did there flash the memory of all those occasions in days gone by

when he might have given this young man a
slosh on the side of the head and had refrained.
And now it was too late. He winced beneath the
bitterness of the might-have-been.

"None of your sauce, if you please," was all
he could find to say.

Syd eyed him sternly.

"Don't you talk back at me! And call me
'm'lord.' I've 'ad to speak to you about this before."

"I'll call you 'm'lord' when the Court so
orders—and not till then."

Syd chuckled.

"You won't 'ave to wait long . . . what with
Ma's evidence and that portrait up there. And
when the courts 'ave declared me Lord Droitwich, do you know the very first thing I'll do?"

"Yes," exploded the overwrought butler.
"You'll listen to me giving you my notice, young
Syd."

"Yah!" was Syd's reply. And, totally oblivious
of his noble blood, he put his tongue out. Slingsby, his equal in spirit, put his tongue out, too.
And it was in this revolting attitude that Sir
Herbert Bassinger, walking briskly into the
room, found them.

"Good God!" cried Sir Herbert, and paused, appalled at the spectacle.

The two tongues shot in again. Slingsby, with a visible effort, recovered his official dignity.

"I beg your pardon, Sir Herbert," he said.

Sir Herbert waved aside the apology.

"Don't mention it!" he said. "I have no doubt the provocation was extreme. I've felt like doing the same myself—often." He turned to Syd and spoke commandingly. "Now, young man."

Syd looked at him with loathing. Of all the personnel of Langley End, not excluding even Slingsby, he disliked Sir Herbert Bassinger most.

"Well," he said, "what's on *your* mind, Serpent?"

Prudently, perhaps, Sir Herbert decided not to hear the last word.

"I want this room. Mr. Wetherby, my lawyer, is coming here."

"The good old conference, eh? What ho!"

"Of course, if you insist on remaining, we must take him to the library."

Syd rose.

"Oh, don't bother. We Droitwiches can do the civil thing. I'll go. But you're just wasting your time and money, you know. What good's a lawyer going to do you when the Court sees me and 'im together?" He jerked a thumb at the portrait of Long-Sword. "Look 'ere," he said, striking an attitude, "upon that picture and on this." He tapped his chest. "Come to think of it, I'd better subpœna that portrait. Make sure it's present in court when the time comes. Well, toodle-oo!"

He passed through the French window. Slingsby gazed after him bulbously.

"Really, Sir 'Erbert," he said brokenly, "I could almost wish he would win his case, so I shouldn't 'ave to go about thinking he was a nephew of mine."

Sir Herbert did not actually pat his faithful servitor on the back, because that sort of thing is not done; but he bestowed upon him a lively and encouraging look.

"That's all right, Slingsby. He isn't going to win the case—not if we play our cards properly. Has Mrs. Price arrived?"

"Yes, Sir Herbert. Roberts brought her down in the Rolls-Royce half an hour ago. She's in my pantry."

"That young man doesn't know she's here?"

"No, Sir Herbert."

"He mustn't," said the baronet emphatically. "He mustn't so much as suspect she's anywhere near the place. Lord Droitwich come yet?"

"Yes, Sir Herbert. I saw his lordship walking in the garden with Miss Brown."

"Miss Brown?" Sir Herbert's eyebrows rose. "The manicure girl?"

"Yes, Sir Herbert."

"What did he want to bring her for?"

"I could not say, Sir Herbert."

A possible theory occurred to Sir Herbert Bassinger.

"She was the first one to hear the old woman's story. Perhaps he thinks her testimony . . . well, never mind. Go and fetch him. And when I ring, bring Mrs. Price in."

"Very good, Sir Herbert."

The butler withdrew. Sir Herbert, left alone, walked slowly across to the mantelpiece and gazed up at the portrait of Long-Sword. He rubbed his chin thoughtfully, and some of the animation left his face. There *was* a resemblance, dash it!

Voices outside warned him of the approach of his wife and the family solicitor.

Chapter Twenty-two

Syd's description of Mr. J. G. Wetherby, of the legal firm of Polk, Wetherby, Polk & Polk, as an old bloke with a face like a halibut had been, if not entirely justified, at any rate reasonably close to the mark. The solicitor was well stricken in years, and his large, glassy eyes, peering through their spectacles, did suggest those of some kind of fish. He came in now in that wary manner peculiar to lawyers, looking from side to side as if expecting to see torts hiding behind the curtains and misdemeanours under the piano.

"Ah, come in, Wetherby," said Sir Herbert, suspending his scrutiny of Long-Sword. "You'll like this better than the library. More sunshine."

Mr. Wetherby inspected the sunshine in a rather suspicious manner, as if warning it to be up to no tricks with him.

"A most pleasant room," he agreed.

Lady Lydia shivered.

"Not to me," she said. "It was here that it all happened."

"Indeed?"

"Well, sit down, Wetherby," said Sir Herbert. "I've sent for Lord Droitwich."

"Yes, let's call him that while we can" said Lady Lydia.

"Ah, here he is. My dear fellow," said Sir Herbert affectionately, hurrying to the window to greet the incoming Tony. "Splendid that you were able to get here."

"Hullo, Aunt Lydia . . . if I may still call you that?"

"You may," said Lady Lydia emphatically.

"How do you do, Mr. Wetherby. I hope I'm not late," said Tony. "I was showing Polly Brown the gardens."

Sir Herbert nodded.

"Ah, yes. It was thoughtful of you to bring Miss Brown, Tony, but I'm sure Wetherby will tell us that her testimony is of no real value. . . . Now, then, Wetherby, we can begin. We're all here."

"Where's Freddie?" Tony asked.

"Still in London. Staying with his friend Tubby Bridgnorth. I telephoned to him to come, but he babbled something about important business. Now, then, Wetherby, there's no need for a lot of preamble. What the devil are we to do?"

Mr. Wetherby put the tips of his fingers together.

"Allow me just to run over my facts," he said. "This old woman signed a paper specifically denying that there was any truth in her story?"

"Yes."

"It was duly witnessed?"

"Yes."

"And Lord Droitwich burned it?"

"Yes."

"And if," said Lady Lydia, with a hard look at Tony, "there is any justice in the world, that ought to be accepted as legal proof that he *is* Lord Droitwich. His father was just the same sort of lunatic."

Tony grinned amiably. Mr. Wetherby turned the searchlight of his spectacles on him.

"May I inquire, Lord Droitwich, *why* you burned that paper?"

"Mr. Wetherby," said Tony, "you may. And

I will answer like a little man. If I hadn't, I should have had to marry Violet Waddington. As it is, I'm going to marry Polly Brown."

If the actual burning of the paper had come as a bombshell to Sir Herbert and Lady Lydia Bassinger, this frank explanation of the motives behind the conflagration proved scarcely less disintegrating.

"Tony!"

"You're crazy!"

Tony had not made the announcement with any expectation of finding it well received. He had foreseen this attitude. Kind hearts might be more than coronets and simple faith than Norman blood, but not, he was aware, in the eyes of Sir Herbert and Lady Lydia Bassinger. Dearly as he loved them, he was not blind to the fact that their mental outlook had a certain inelasticity. They belonged to the more old-fashioned type of aristocrat, and had not acquired that easy modern casualness where birth was concerned. He prepared to be firm.

"Nonsense," he said genially. "You like her. You know you do."

Lady Lydia would have none of this reasoning. It was quite true—and she would not have denied it—that she did like Polly. But it is perfectly possible to esteem a working girl quite warmly without being ready to accept her as the wife of the head of the family.

"Our likes and dislikes are not the point," she said. "The thing's impossible."

"Quite," agreed Sir Herbert.

Mr. Wetherby said nothing. He merely polished a finger-nail with the corner of his handkerchief.

"Why?" asked Tony.

"A manicure girl!"

"A most suitable match for a barber. As Syd was pointing out only just now."

"It's out of the question . . ." Sir Herbert was beginning when Tony interrupted him.

"Now, listen, you two dear old things," said Tony, "I expected a little consternation, but don't overdo it. This marriage is going through. If I've had the luck to win the love of a girl like Polly, you can bet your boots I'm not going to be such a mug as to chuck it away."

"But suppose the courts decide that you are Lord Droitwich?"

"In that case," said Tony, "the family will be

one Lady Droitwich to the good on the general score."

Sir Herbert looked at Lady Lydia. Lady Lydia looked at Sir Herbert. They both looked at Mr. Wetherby, but got no satisfaction from him, for he had just begun to polish another finger-nail. Family solicitors always achieve an admirable detachment on these occasions. Physically, Mr. Wetherby was still present. Spiritually, his manner suggested, he was a hundred miles away.

"Didn't I say he was crazy?" cried Lady Lydia.

Tony maintained an unruffled composure. He was sorry for these two sufferers, but he intended to yield not an inch.

"Now, come, darling," he urged, "you know you aren't really as upset as all that. Pure swank, that's what it is. Stop behaving like an aunt and let's see that merry smile of yours once more. You know you liked Polly when you met her, and you know that when you've seen a little more of her you'll love her as much as I do."

"I know nothing of the kind."

"Then you'll have to try to learn to," said Tony. He prepared to play his trump card.

"I'm sorry to hold a pistol to your heads," he went on, "but, if you're going to be the stern old aristocrats, all bets are off. If the family is not prepared to accept Polly, I walk straight out, leaving the field to Syd. Would you rather have Polly as a countess or Syd as an earl?" He paused to allow of the digestion of this shattering remark. "I'll leave you to think it over," he said, walking to the window. "As Syd observed on a certain memorable occasion, I'll give you ten minutes by my Ingersoll."

A stunned silence followed his departure. Once more, Sir Herbert and his wife exchanged glances. Each found in the other's a total absence of optimism.

"He means it," said Sir Herbert.

"Yes," said Lady Lydia.

"And he's as obstinate as the devil."

"Yes," said Lady Lydia again. "His father was just the same."

"Old Price?" cried Mr. Wetherby, surprised. He had not intended to enter the conversation until called upon, but this statement had startled him out of his reserve.

"No," said Lady Lydia. "My brother John."

She sighed. "How all this brings back the time when he wanted to marry the barmaid!"

Sir Herbert had succeeded in pulling himself together.

"Well, we've enough to worry about," he declared, "without bothering ourselves as to who or when or what Tony marries. The immediate problem before us is, How are we to tackle Mrs. Price?"

Mr. Wetherby was now his old alert self again. This was the matter that immediately concerned him, and he addressed himself to it with that senile vigour which lawyers always display when you stir them up.

"To me," he said briskly, "it is obvious that we must induce her to sign another paper."

"Exactly," agreed Sir Herbert. "And you're the man to work it, Wetherby. Your arguments will have more weight than ours."

"She wouldn't listen to us," added Lady Lydia. "Herbert appealed to her better nature five times before we left London—and she hadn't any."

"The difficulty," Sir Herbert explained, "as far as I can make out, is that she is intensely superstitious and took the burning of that paper, in consequence, as a sort of omen. A kind of sign from heaven to show her the right path."

"So now," said Lady Lydia, "we want you to convince her that heaven has sent her down a wrong turning."

"I feel sure you can handle her, Wetherby. She's quite an ignorant old woman. If you are curt . . . and rather sinister . . . and—well, *you* know . . . *legal* . . ."

Mr. Wetherby nodded understandingly. He would never have put it so colloquially, but what he was feeling was that this was right up his street.

"Quite, quite. I interpret your meaning exactly. It might be as well if I were to draw up the necessary document now, that we may have it in readiness."

He rose and was making for the desk when he perceived that their little company had been increased. An immaculate figure had sauntered through the door and was being greeted by its nearest and dearest.

"Freddie!" cried Sir Herbert. "I thought you said you wouldn't be here."

The Hon. Freddie nodded.

"Changed my mind," he explained briefly. "Hullo, Aunt Lydia."

"Good-morning, Freddie. You know Mr. Wetherby?"

"Rather! 'Morning, Mr. Wetherby. You're looking very bonny. How," asked Freddie, "are all the little torts and replevins to-day?"

The lawyer smiled a bleak smile and seated himself at the desk. Inspiration had evidently descended upon him, for his pen began to scratch immediately.

Lady Lydia resumed her conversation with her nephew.

"What made you decide to come, after all?"

"The most startling and momentous happening. Where's Tony?"

Lady Lydia indicated the garden.

"Out there, somewhere. With," she added a little tonelessly, "his fiancée."

"Eh?" Freddie stared. "But didn't I understand that Violet had handed him his hat and returned him to store?"

"Yes. This is a new one. Miss Polly Brown."

Freddie's enthusiasm was unstinted.

"You don't mean to tell me Tony's teamed up

with that delightful, ripping little girl? Excellent work! Oh, very excellent work!"

"I'm glad you're pleased!"

"And I'll bet *he* is," said Freddie. "And I've a bit of news for him that'll make him more pleased still. Send him singing about the house."

Sir Herbert, during these remarks, had been engaged in pressing the bell. He now came back, interested.

"What news?" he asked.

His nephew regarded him stonily.

"Never mind," he said. "It is for Tony's ears alone. If you'll forgive me saying so, Uncle Herbert, you've the makings in you of a very fine Nosey Parker."

And, wagging a reproving finger, the Hon. Freddie dashed out of the French window.

Lady Lydia looked after him and shrugged her shoulders.

"Eccentric family!" she murmured.

The door opened, and Slingsby appeared.

"You rang, Sir Herbert?"

"Mrs. Price," said the baronet.

"I brought her when I heard the bell, Sir Herbert."

"Is she outside?"

"On the mat, Sir Herbert."

"Bring her in. And stay yourself. We shall need a witness."

Mr. Wetherby had risen, a paper in his hand.

"Finished?" said Sir Herbert.

The lawyer handed him the document.

"Brief but adequate, I think?"

"Excellent," said Sir Herbert, reading.

The door opened again. Slingsby, who had left the room for an instant, returned, shepherding before him the black-satined figure of Ma Price.

Chapter Twenty-three

MA PRICE was intensely sober and very apprehensive. She deeply mistrusted the look of things. She was a woman who, like some ancient Greek or Roman, was accustomed to rule her life in accordance with signs and omens; and when Tony had burned her statement that afternoon in the barber-shop she had regarded the action, as Sir Herbert Bassinger had explained to Mr. Wetherby, in the light of a broad hint from above that in signing that document she had done the wrong thing and had better be very careful in future.

In this faith she had held firm against all arguments and entreaties for a full two weeks; and then, just as she had become convinced that she was working along the right lines, along came another portent in the shape of a black

cat, which crossed her path halfway down Mott
Street, when she was on her way to the Caterpillar and Jug. And now she didn't know where
she was.

In the matter of black cats, the opinion of
the public is sharply divided. One school of
thought regards them as harbingers of good
fortune; a second as a sign of impending
calamity. And there is a third and smaller group
which holds them to be a warning. It was to this
section that Ma Price belonged. She did not
yet know what she was being warned against,
but she felt she had been warned.

Her manner, therefore, as she entered the
room, was a compound of gloom and wariness.
She looked like a female Daniel diffidently
entering a den of lions.

"Ah, come in, Mrs. Price," said Sir Herbert.

"Yes, Sir Rerbert," responded Daniel, eyeing
this leading lion nervously.

"Take a seat," said Lady Lydia, with a look
of loathing and an inflection in her voice which
suggested that she would have preferred to offer
her visitor a cup of hemlock.

"Thank you, Lady Lidgier."

"This," said Sir Herbert, "is **Mr. Wetherby,**
the family solicitor."

Ma Price, who had seated herself on the extreme edge of a chair with infinite caution, half
rose and bobbed agitatedly. Her sense of impending doom deepened. A voracious reader of
the *Family Herald* and similar publications,
she knew all about family solicitors. They were
never up to any good. They destroyed wills, kid-
napped heirs, and had even been known to mur-
der baronets. She suspected Mr. Wetherby from
the outset; and, wriggling in her chair, looked
plaintively at her hostess.

"Could I 'ave a drop of port, your ladyship?"

"No!"

"Oh, very well," said Ma Price, sniffing disconsolately.

"You see," said Sir Herbert blandly, "this is
not a feast or festival to which we have bidden
you, Mrs. Price. More in the nature of a business conference. You shall have your port later."

"Thank you, Sir Rerbert."

"Meanwhile, Mr. Wetherby wishes to ask you
a few questions."

"Yes, Sir Rerbert," said Ma Price, in the
depths.

"Now, Wetherby," said Sir Herbert.

At these words, Mr. Wetherby, who had been polishing his spectacles, put them on and uttered a single, dry, sharp, short, sinister cough. Its rasping note caused the star witness to quiver from stem to stern like a jelly. It did not need the lawyer's eyes, peering over the spectacles, to inform her that this was the bugle note that sounded the attack. If Mr. Wetherby had emitted a loud hunting-cry, he could not have indicated more clearly that the proceedings proper were about to begin.

"Mrs. Price," said the lawyer.

"Yes, sir?"

"You appear apprehensive."

" 'Pear what, sir?"

"Mr. Wetherby," interpreted Sir Herbert, "means that you seem nervous."

"Not nervous, exactly, Sir Rerbert. But what with havin' a uniformed chauffeur sent for me and the luxury of ridin' in a Rolls-Royce and all, me 'ead's swimmin'."

"I see. Well, calm yourself, Mrs. Price. You have nothing to fear, provided . . . eh, Wetherby?"

"Quite," assented the lawyer. "Provided she tells the truth."

"The whole truth," said Lady Lydia.

"And nothing but the truth."

"So 'elp me Gawd," muttered Ma Price automatically, raising a trembling hand.

Sir Herbert shot a glance at the lawyer.

"And—er—signs a document to that effect?" he said.

"Quite," said Mr. Wetherby.

"Quite," said Sir Herbert.

"Quite," said Mr. Wetherby again, clinching the thing.

A pause followed this exchange of remarks. The two men and Lady Lydia looked at one another significantly. As for Ma Price, she had edged into her chair like a tortoise into its shell. All these "Quites," whistling about her head had reduced her to a protoplasmic condition.

Her *sang-froid* was not restored by another rasping cough from Mr. Wetherby.

"Now, Mrs. Price."

"Yes, sir?"

The lawyer peered over his spectacles.

"It has been brought to my attention," he said in a cold, menacing voice, "that you are respon-

sible for an astounding story, tending to cast
doubt upon the present Lord Droitwich's right
to hold his title and estates."

Of the thirty-one words in this speech, Ma
Price had understood perhaps seven. However,
"Yes, sir" seemed to be the right answer, so
she made it.

"You assert that, being placed in charge of
Lord Droitwich in his infancy, you substituted
for him your own baby, and that the real Lord
Droitwich is the young man who until now has
been called Syd Price?"

"Yes, sir."

"Tell me, Mrs. Price, are you subject to hal-
lucinations?"

Ma Price missed this one by a mile.

"Sir?" she said, fogged.

"Shall I say, have you a vivid imagination?"

"I dunno, sir."

"I think you have, Mrs. Price," said the
lawyer, growing every moment more like a gentlemanly boa constrictor hypnotizing its prey.
"And I put it to you . . . I put it to you, Mrs.
Price . . . that this story of yours is simply
and solely—from start to finish—a figment of
the imagination."

"What's a figment?" asked Ma Price guardedly.

Mr. Wetherby uttered another of his coughs, supplementing it this time by rapping in a sinister manner on the desk with the edge of his spectacle case.

"I would like to ask you a few questions," he said. "Are you a great reader, Mrs. Price?"

"Yes, sir."

"Were you a great reader—shall we say, sixteen years ago?"

"Yes, sir."

"Of what type of literature?"

"I liked me *Family Herald.*"

"Ah! And did you often go to the theatre in those days?"

"If there was a good melodrama, I did."

"Quite! Now, attend to me, Mrs. Price. May I remind you that this changing of one baby for another of greater rank has been the basis of a hundred *Family Herald* novelettes, and is such a stock situation of melodrama that the late W. S. Gilbert satirized it in his poem, 'The Baby's Vengeance'?"

"What are you getting at?"

"I will tell you what I am 'getting at.' I suggest to you that your story is nothing but a fairy tale arising from too much *Family Herald,* too much melodrama, and—may I say—too much unsweetened gin?"

"Precisely!" said Sir Herbert.

"Exactly!" said Lady Lydia.

They gave the impression of having with difficulty restrained themselves from cheering.

It had taken Ma Price a moment or two to assimilate the insult in all its bearings, but now it penetrated, and she rose militantly, her hands on her hips.

" 'Ere!" she began.

"Sit down," said Mr. Wetherby.

"Yes, sir," said Ma Price meekly.

"We now come," proceeded Mr. Wetherby, "to another point. Two weeks ago, you signed a document denying that there was any truth in your story."

"Yes, sir. It got itself burned."

"I am aware of that. And so I have prepared another, similar document. Will you kindly step this way, Mrs. Price?"

He indicated the desk.

"Here is a pen, Mrs. Price. Sign there, if you please."

"Slingsby," said Sir Herbert.

The butler stepped forward.

"Witness Mrs. Price's signature."

"Very good, Sir Herbert."

"You see, Mrs. Price," said Mr. Wetherby, "it is essential for your own sake that you sign this document which I have prepared. Should you decline to do so, you will be placed in a very unfortunate position when you go into the witness box. Counsel will undoubtedly ask why, if you were willing to swear to a certain truth once, you refused to do so when asked to again. Perjury is a very serious offense, Mrs. Price."

"Perjury!"

"Perjury is what I said."

Ma Price was convinced. She understood now the significance of that black cat. It had been sent to warn her of the peril in which she stood. But for it, she might have gone unheedingly on her way, only to meet disaster in the end. She took up the pen with the emotions of one who has had a merciful escape; and Mr. Wetherby, relaxing in this moment of triumph, removed his spectacles and began to polish them again.

Ma Price rose and approached the desk. It

stood by the window, and through the window, as she advanced, her eyes fell on the pleasant lawns and shrubberies without. And suddenly, as if riveted by some sinister sight, they glared intently. She had picked up the pen. She now threw it from her with a clatter.

"Coo!" she cried.

Sir Herbert jumped.

"What the devil is it now?" he demanded irritably.

Ma Price turned and faced them resolutely. The sight she had just seen had brought it home to her that she had been all wrong in her diagnosis of the black cat. It had been sent to warn her—yes, but to warn her against signing the paper. Otherwise, why, as her fingers clutched the pen, should this other portent have been presented, as if for good measure?

"I'm not going to sign!"

"What! !"

"I'm not!"

"Why not?" cried Lady Lydia.

Ma Price pointed dramatically at the window.

"I just seen a magpie!" she said.

Chapter Twenty-four

W HEN, in a drawing room of reasonable proportions, a family solicitor is exclaiming "Absurd!"; a baronet, "Confound the woman!"; his wife, "Insane!"; and the widow of a Knightsbridge barber, "I tell you I seen a magpie!"— all simultaneously, there is bound to be a confused babel of sound, distressing to the ear of anyone entering the room at the moment.

Syd found it so. He had come in at the exact instant when the uproar was at its height, and he felt as he had sometimes felt at stormy meetings of the Fulham Debating Society when passions ran high and half a dozen Honourable Members were endeavouring to ventilate their grievances at the same time. He looked about him peevishly. He had done the gentlemanly thing, he considered, in allowing these plotters to conduct their plotting in his own house, and the least they could do in return was to plot quietly.

"Oy!" he bellowed in a voice like a foghorn.

The tumult died away. He surveyed the gathering coldly.

"My Gawd!" he said, with bitterness. "Call this a conference? More like the parrot 'ouse at the Zoo."

The intrusion of this alien and subversive influence at such a moment affected Sir Herbert Bassinger profoundly.

"Get out of here!" thundered Sir Herbert.

Syd quelled him with a glance.

"Less of it, Viper," he said curtly.

And then, for the first time, his gaze fell on Ma Price, and he stood, bewildered.

"Ma! You 'ere?"

Ma Price was in emotional mood.

"Oh, Syd," she cried, "I seen it just in time!"

"Seen what?"

"The magpie. It was sent. Another second and I'd have signed the paper."

"Paper?" A sudden blinding light shone upon Syd. "Jiminy Christmas!" he exclaimed, stunned. *"More* tampering!" He turned on Sir Herbert, aglow with righteous indignation. "Of all the slippery, slithery 'uman eels," he said shrilly, "you cop the biscuit! I've only to take me eye off you for a 'alf a tick and you're up to your old games. It's enough to drive a fellow silly." He swung round and pointed an accusing finger at Mr. Wetherby. "'Ere, you with the face. Call yourself a lawyer? Lending yourself to these goings-on? I've a good mind to report you to the Lord Chancellor or whoever it is and have you struck off the Rolls."

Lady Lydia appealed to her masculine allies. The situation seemed to her to be beyond the scope of a frail woman.

"Is there no way of removing this appalling young man?" she moaned.

"No, there ain't," said Syd. "Not till I've done what I come to do."

He turned to the door, as Wellington might have turned to his troops at Waterloo when giving the order for the whole line to advance.

"Fetch in that ladder!" he said.

And Charles, the footman, entered, carrying with some difficulty a short ladder, at which Sir Herbert stared, completely at a loss.

"What the devil are you up to now?" demanded Sir Herbert.

Syd pointed at the portrait of Long-Sword above the mantelpiece.

"Sub-pœna-ing His Nibs," he said. "Crikey! That portrait ain't *safe* 'ere. First thing I know, if I don't take it away, you'll be painting a new face on it."

He took the other end of the ladder and moved resolutely towards the mantelpiece. Footman Charles, who would have been the first to admit that he did not know what all this was about but who was having the time of his life, moved with him, a docile ally. Charles was of an age to enjoy family rows. This one looked like culminating in mayhem; and if it culminated in mayhem that was all right with Charles.

To Slingsby, on the other hand, a seasoned butler, the whole thing from its inception had been monstrous and saddening. In all his eleven years of butlerhood, nobody had ever brought ladders into the drawing room before. His blood was afire, and only an innate respect for the Family had kept him from plunging actively into the scene. Usually, he did not speak till spoken to, but at a time like this all recognized rules go by the board.

"Is it your wish, Sir Herbert," he asked, panting a little with emotion, "that the portrait be removed?"

"Certainly not!" cried Lady Lydia.

"Of course not," boomed Sir Herbert. "Take that damned ladder out of here!"

Mr. Wetherby did not speak. But he looked at Syd in a sinister, legal sort of way, as much as to inform him that the test case of Rex v. Winterbotham, Gooch, and Simms, Merryweather intervening, covered the present situation and that he had better be careful.

Syd was not to be intimidated by word or by look. He knew his rights and meant to stick up for them.

"I'm going to show that picture in court. It'll 'elp my case, and I mean to 'ave it."

Ma Price, like Charles, was foggy as to what exactly all this was about, but she felt that a word in season could do no harm.

"Oh, Syd," she said. "Don't be so 'asty."

Syd waved her down imperiously.

"Cheese it, Ma. Here, give that to me," he exclaimed with sudden fury. For Slingsby, an active force at last, had pushed him away and caused him to loosen his grip on the ladder. He made a dive to recover it, and Slingsby and

Charles, the latter now definitely beaming, lifted it over his head.

He uttered a stricken cry.

"Now you've made me walk under a ladder! Just as my case is going to be tried, too!"

The disaster seemed to remove from him the last vestiges of self-control. Nobody could spend a lifetime in the society of Ma Price without developing a superstitious trend of thought, and the unfortunate incident had moved him deeply. It gave him the impression that not only the seen but the unseen world was against him. Berserk, he clutched forcefully at the butler's coat-tails, and with this gesture the Battle of the Ladder may be said to have begun.

It was essentially a scene of action, in which it would have been unreasonable to expect anything in the nature of sparkling dialogue from those involved. Mr. Wetherby clicked his tongue and said that all this was most irregular. Ma Price exclaimed, "Syd, dearie!" And Slingsby shouted, "Let go of me, you young ruffian!" But, apart from this, a grim silence prevailed, broken only by the hard breathing of the combatants and the occasional cry of the wounded.

Above the fray, Long-Sword looked down—
it seemed approvingly. Many was the time
Long-Sword had been mixed up in this sort of
free-for-all. If he had a criticism to offer, it
was probably a regret that there was no battle-
axe-work. Apart from that, he had nothing to
suggest. The affair had begun to develop on the
most satisfactory lines, for now Sir Herbert
Bassinger had been drawn into the battle-swirl.

At the beginning of the struggle, Sir Herbert
had stood aloof, contenting himself with word
and gesture. But now a swift turn on the part
of Slingsby caused the ladder to revolve in his
direction. Syd shifted his hold from the butler's
coat to the ladder itself. It swung menacingly
at the Baronet's waistcoat, and he pushed it
away. Slingsby and Charles gave a quick hoist
and then pulled downwards. This placed Sir
Herbert in jeopardy once more. To avoid being
hit on the shins, he leaped like a young lamb in
springtime and, descending, found himself with
one leg between the rungs. In this position he
hopped madly.

"Stop it!" bellowed Sir Herbert. "Can't you see
you're pulling me apart? Stop it! I'm caught!"

The butler heard the voice of authority, and

was not deaf to its pleadings. With a mighty
effort he jerked the ladder down. It swung
sharply outwards, and Syd, being in its path,
dropped like corn before the sickle.

"Let me out!"

The ladder fell. Sir Herbert fell into a chair,
clutching his foot.

"Hell and blazes!" cried Sir Herbert, in
agony. "My gouty toe, too!" He glared at Syd.
"It's all your fault, you confounded hooligan."

Mere verbal censure could not hurt Syd now.
He had passed that phase. He was clasping his
stomach and rocking agitatedly.

"If any of my innards are knocked out of
place," he stated, "I'll 'ave the law on the blooming lot of you!"

Sir Herbert turned to Slingsby. Doom was in
his face.

"Slingsby, will you see this young man off the
premises as quickly as possible."

A beatific smile came into the butler's care-
worn face.

"Beg pardon, could I hear that again, Sir
Herbert?"

"See," said Lady Lydia, "that he is packed
up and shown the way to the Park gates."

"Yes, m'lady. Thank *you,* m'lady."

Licking his lips, the butler examined the toe of his right shoe for a moment; then, clenching and unclenching his hands, he advanced upon Syd.

Syd backed towards the window.

"Now, then!" he urged. "No violence!"

Ma Price threw herself in the path of vengeance.

"Theodore! Don't you dare to touch him!"

"Out of the way, Bella."

"I've warned you," said Syd nervously, continuing his retreat. Then, as the butler's advance became too menacing to be endured, he made a sudden bolt for the window; and, doing so, collided heavily with Tony, who, followed by Freddie and Polly, was at that moment coming in.

Tony caught Syd neatly and bounced him back into the room.

"Football season's begun early this year, hasn't it?" he said, puzzled. He looked from Slingsby, who was breathing heavily and seemed as if at any instant he might begin exhaling fire, to Syd, who had taken refuge behind the sofa and was standing there poising a heavy vase in mingled defense and defiance. "What's it all about?"

Sir Herbert answered the question.

"Only Lord Droitwich proving his gentle birth by brawling with the butler."

Syd was gruffly apologetic.

"P'r'aps I *was* wrong to get my monkey up, but I saw red."

"You look red," said Freddie.

"I don't suppose I'm the first Droitwich to make a mistake."

"No," agreed Sir Herbert. "If you *are* a Droitwich, your father made a big one."

Syd was wounded. He addressed himself to Ma Price.

" 'Ear that?" He turned to Sir Herbert. "In the face of extreme provication," he said with dignity, "I've done me best to keep on friendly terms with you and Aunt Lydia, but it don't seem to be any use."

"But what's the trouble about?" asked Tony.

Sir Herbert snorted. His recent experiences had left him ruffled. The pain in his toe had begun to abate, but his feelings were still outraged.

"He was trying to remove the Pourbous."

"I wasn't," said Syd heatedly. "All I was after was that picture up there."

"The name of the artist who painted the portrait of Long-Sword," said Lady Lydia, with frigid scorn, "was Pourbous."

"Oh?" Syd seemed to digest this. "Well, 'ave it your own way."

Tony looked puzzled.

"What did you want old Long-Sword for?" he asked.

"So as there shouldn't be any tamperin' with him. I didn't want his face altered before I got him into court. Ma," said Syd, waving his hand, "take a squint at that old josser and tell me who he reminds you of."

"Well . . ."

"Is he like me or isn't he?" demanded Syd impatiently.

Ma Price peered at the portrait.

"It certainly does look like you, dearie."

"He hasn't quite got my expression. The determination, I mean. Maybe he had it, and old Porpoise the painter didn't put it in. Still, my lawyers think that old bloke is going to 'elp me a lot, and I don't intend to have any serpents tamperin' with him."

Tony laughed.

"Is that all that's troubling you? You needn't worry. I'll see that Long-Sword is in court to witness the struggle, complete with face as at present."

"Well!" said Syd, impressed. "You may be a barber's son, but, blimey, you fight like a gentleman. I suppose you know that picture is going to dish you properly? What I mean, if Ma sticks to her evidence the way she's going to."

"Very likely."

Syd seemed a little bewildered.

"Don't you *want* to win the case?" he asked.

"Well, honestly," said Tony, "after hearing Freddie's news, I admit I'm wavering. You see, if I win, I shall be Lord Droitwich . . ."

"You won't win."

"And if I don't—meet Price, the well-to-do millionaire."

"What on earth," demanded Sir Herbert peevishly, "are you talking about?"

"Tell them, Freddie."

The Hon. Freddie stepped forward with his customary grace.

Chapter Twenty-five

THERE was always in the demeanour of the Hon. Freddie Chalk-Marshall, when mingling with his fellow men, the suggestion that he looked upon himself as the only responsible adult in a gathering of half-witted children. This now had become subtly intensified. He surveyed the little group before him with a fatherly eye. He seemed to be saying that, if only people would leave everything to him, there would never be any bother or trouble whatsoever.

He cleared his throat, shot his cuffs, and began to speak.

"I don't know," he said, glancing round the company as if to ascertain whether or not he was testing their intelligence too exactingly, "if any of you birds ever read poetry?"

Sir Herbert, who was not at his calmest, made

a noise like a gramophone needle slipping off a record, and suggested with an asperity which he did not try to conceal that the speaker should come to the point. It was a piece of heckling which might have disturbed a less composed orator, but Freddie merely threw a chilly look in his uncle's direction.

"I'm coming to the point all right. My remark about poetry, you will find before you're much older and fatter, was essentially germane to the issue. I was about to say that, if you did, you might have come across a little thing of somebody's which runs as follows: 'Full many a gem of purest ray serene,'" said Freddie, "'the dark, unfathomed caves of ocean bear. Full many a flower is born to blush unseen and waste its sweetness . . .'"

"Oh, good Lord!"

"'. . . on the desert air,'" added Freddie severely.

It was Sir Herbert, still unquelled, who had made the interruption. Lady Lydia, like a loyal wife, supported him.

"You're quite right, Herbert. Freddie darling," said Lady Lydia plaintively, "is all this really necessary? I mean, we can listen to you reciting at any time."

"Aunt Lydia," replied Freddie, more gently than when dealing with his uncle, for he had no wish to be hard on women, "would it be asking too much to entreat you to switch it off for just about half a minute? I cannot continue if my flesh and blood are going to butt in every two seconds. Go into the silence, will you?"

"Oh, all right."

Freddie resumed.

"Now, why, you will ask, were those gems and flowers in the position described? Why did they never top the bill? What prevented them from pulling their weight and making a name for themselves? They were good gems, excellent flowers. And yet they were simply a total loss. Why? I will tell you. It was because they hadn't a knowledgeable bloke with a genius for salesmanship behind them, shoving them along. Mere merit is nothing without salesmanship. It's no good having an A 1 gem, if you don't know how to exploit it. That goes for flowers, too. And the same applies to hair restorers."

Again Sir Herbert seemed about to speak, but he met his nephew's eye and refrained.

"Many years ago," proceeded Freddie, "a fellow invented a dashed good hair restorer. What it contained, I cannot tell you. A little of this, no doubt, and a little of that. He called it Price's Derma Vitalis."

Syd had been sitting with his chin cupped in his hands and his eyes fixed on the portrait of Long-Sword, as if he feared to take them off lest some sort of tampering might ensue. Now, for the first time, he showed interest.

"What's that?" he asked. "What's that about Price's Derma Vitalis?"

"Unless Freddie intends to recite a few more poems first," said Tony encouragingly, "you will soon hear. His story is a sizzler. If any of you have weak hearts, hold onto something. Freddie, give us 'Gunga Din' and 'The Charge of the Light Brigade' and then get down to facts."

Freddie declined to be hustled.

"Price's Derma Vitalis," he said, "was always a potential winner, but there was nobody to get behind it and push. Old Price appears to have bottled it in a desultory sort of way and sold an odd specimen or two to his clients, but for years there was nothing in the nature of what you might call real activity. Then I came along. I saw there was a fortune in the stuff, if properly handled. I decided to put it on the map. There it was, blushing unseen in the dark, unfathomed caves of Mott Street, Knightsbridge, and I took hold."

He held his audience with a burning eye.

"I took hold," he repeated. "My first, action was to send half a dozen bottles to Tubby Bridgnorth's American father-in-law-to-be, having previously ascertained from an authoritative source that he was bald to the core. I gave him a sales talk at lunch. 'Just try it,' I said. 'That's all I ask. No harm in *trying* the dashed stuff, is there?' A very reasonable old bird, Tubby's future father-in-law. I am not surprised that he has amassed wealth. He has the open mind that wins to success. He saw my point. He tried the Derma Vitalis. And now, a bare two weeks later, there has appeared on his egg-like cupola something that looks like the faint beginnings of a young door mat."

A feverish exclamation burst from Syd. He was deeply moved.

"If this is true," said Syd, awed, "the name of Price'll go down in 'istory."

"And now," concluded Freddie, "a company

is to be formed with a view to exploiting the stuff internationally, and they've sent me to find Tony and get him to name a figure. And old Beamish says you can make it as stiff as you like, Tony, because the shares are to be placed on the American market and, by some process which I do not pretend to follow, it will be the mugs who will pay. I believe this is always the case in matters of high finance."

Syd had risen. He was staring as one who sees visions.

"Coo! I'll ask a hundred thousand—blessed if I don't."

A derisive laugh shot like a bullet from Freddie. It stopped Syd in mid-stride, as he feverishly paced the room. He turned, belligerent and suspicious. Sudden laughter always affected Syd unpleasantly.

"What are you cackling about?" he asked.

"Only at the idea of your talking terms to old Beamish. My poor ass, what the dickens have you got to do with it?"

"Eh?"

"The stuff." explained Freddie, "belongs to Tony."

As the significance of the words penetrated,

Syd's jaw fell slowly, and a dull flush spread over his face.

"Ho! Think you can rob me of my birthright, do you?"

"It isn't your birthright."

"Exactly," agreed Sir Herbert. "You can't have both ways, young man. If you're Lord Droitwich, you can have no possible connection with Price's—whatever he called it."

There was a weighty pause. Syd appeared to be thinking. Then, with a suddenness which drew from her a terrified "Ow!" he seized Ma Price by the wrist and manœuvred her to the desk like a tug pushing an ocean liner. He picked up the pen and thrust it in her hand.

"That paper, Ma! You sign it—and quick!"

"But, Syd . . ."

"Yes, *Syd!*" cried the Claimant. "Syd it is, and Syd it's going to be. Syd Price, sole proprietor of the famous Derma Vitalis—that's me." He glared at the family group. "You think I want to be a measly earl now that this has happened? A fat chance!" He took the paper and thrust it in his pocket. "I'm going to stick to this," he said, "in case you ever try any funny business. If ever any of you come trying to start anything about me being Lord Droitwich, I'll 'ave this paper to show, duly signed by Ma, as evidence that it's all a lot of poppycock." He moved to the window. "Come on, Ma."

The whirl of events had reduced Ma Price to the condition which she would have described as not knowing whether she stood on her heels or her head. Her mind was a mere jumble of black cats, magpies, coughing lawyers, and documents.

" 'Ave I done right?" asked Ma Price feebly.

"Of course you've done right. And where," said Syd, "you ever got all this nonsense about me bein' an earl into your head is more than I can understand."

He pushed Ma Price out through the French window, then turned for a last thrust.

"If any of you wish to communicate with me in the future, ring up the Ritz!"

Freddie caught his eye.

"Don't forget," he reminded him suavely, "that I scoop in ten per cent commission."

Some of the elation left Syd's face. He regarded Freddie broodingly.

"Coo!" he said, in a wistful voice. "I'd like to 'ave the chance of shavin' you again some day!"

He turned and was gone.

Tony reached for Polly's hand.

"Well, that's that!" he said.

Years seemed to have rolled from Sir Herbert Bassinger. The passing of the shadow had removed from his soul a heavy burden.

"Tony!" His voice almost cracked with emotion. "I congratulate you."

Tony beamed.

"You well may . . . Oh," he said, "you mean about getting the title? I thought you meant because I'm going to marry Polly."

Undeniably there was a moment of discomfort. Some of the burden which had gone from Sir Herbert seemed to return.

"Er . . . h'm . . ." he began.

It was Lady Lydia who rose to the occasion. She was a woman who could face the inevitable. She came to Polly and kissed her. And if there was a sigh behind the kiss, a sigh of regret for that unknown débutante of ancient family and solid wealth who would never now become Lady Droitwich, she did not show it.

"My dear," she said, "I'm sure that Tony is very much to be congratulated."

She turned to Slingsby.

"Go and mix me a cocktail, Slingsby. I need it."

"No!" said Freddie firmly. "On an occasion like this, only one man can mix the cocktails." He tapped his chest: "F. Chalk-Marshall, the man who brought the good news from Aix to Ghent."

"Well, if it poisons me," said Lady Lydia, accompanying him to the door, "I shall die happy."

Slingsby stood aside to let them pass, then followed them out. His moonlike face seemed to glow with inner rapture.

"A cocktail?" said Sir Herbert brightly. "Not a bad idea. Wetherby . . . ?"

"Quite!" said Mr. Wetherby.

Tony kissed his Polly.

"And so at long last," he said, "peace and happiness came to Anthony, fifth Earl of Droitwich. . . ."

Polly had drawn away, and was staring at him miserably.

"Tony, I can't!"

"Can't what?"

"Marry you."

Tony smiled confidently.

"You wait till I get you to St. George's, Hanover Square," he said. "You'll see how quick you can marry me!"

"But this place. It's so big!"

"You'll get used to it."

"But I couldn't be a countess."

"Don't be so dashed superior about countesses," said Tony. "They're just as good as you are."

"But I'm scared!"

"Now, listen," said Tony. "When you accepted me, I was a barber. By industry and enterprise I have worked my way up to being an earl. You can't let me down now. It would be a blow at all ambition. Think of the young men, trying to get on in the world, whom it would discourage. What's the use of sweating to make good, they would say, if your girl's going to chuck you in the hour of triumph?"

"But, Tony . . . can't you see? . . . Don't you understand? . . . I'm not fitted . . . I should be . . ."

"Ah, *come* on!" said Tony briefly.

He put an end to her ramblings by picking her up and carrying her to the door. Here he paused for a moment in order to kiss her.

"Tony and Polly!" he said. "The old firm!"

He kissed her again, and they passed on to where a musical jingling announced that the Hon. Freddie Chalk-Marshall was doing his bit.

THE END